The Center

BREEON'S STORY

WRITTEN BY
D. RENEA

This book is a work of fiction. Names, characters, places and incidents are either the product of the author's imagination or are used fictionally. Any resemblance to actual persons, living or dead, or to actual events or locales is entirely coincidental.

This ebook is licensed for your personal enjoyment only. This ebook may not be re-sold or given away to other people. If you like to share this book with another person, please purchase an additional copy for each person you share it with.

Copyright © 2020 D. Renea All rights reserved. Including the right to reproduce this book or portions thereof, in any form. No part of this text may be reproduced in any form without the express written permission of the author.

Dedication

For every teen keeping a secret, or in a situation and too scared to ask for help...and every adult waiting and willing to do just that.

D. RENEA

Anita Baker blared from the speakers of the blue Chevy Cruze as it glided down the streets of Flint, Michigan. Although the driver, Tiffany "Fab" Grant, was only in her early thirties, she was an old soul and loved music from all different eras and genres. Since she had to be up and at The Center early, it was definitely a "Same Ole Love" kind of morning, and she sang along over the musical legend as she made her way to her destination.

In record time, she pulled into the parking lot of the Toney-Walker Community Center, known only as The Center, and was surprised to see someone sitting on the stairs. It was nearing six in the morning, so the sun was barely up, freezing cold, and The Center didn't open for another four hours. Fab sat in the car for a minute, trying to make out who the person was. After noticing it was a young woman, she grabbed her purse and hesitantly approached

THE CENTER: BREEON'S STORY

them.

Breeon Bennett had been sitting on the stairs of the community center for almost two hours. She couldn't go home, and she didn't have anywhere else to go to get help. Feeling embarrassed and scared, she sat on the stairs of The Center in the dark, waiting for someone to pull up. Seeing Fab immediately sent her into a whirlwind of emotions, and Breeon ran to her, almost hysterical.

"Miss Fab, I need help," Breeon voiced as she met her on the sidewalk.

Fab immediately noticed Breeon looked like she had been into a nasty fight. Her caramel-colored face was bloody, her usually well-maintained hair was all over her head, and one of her eyes were black and swollen shut. Dried blood had stained her nose and lips. Without waiting for a response, Breeon fell into Fab's arms.

"It's okay, Breeon, it's okay. Tell me what's going on," Fab said, wrapping her arms around the teenage girl and unlocking the door before walking her into the building.

The Center was a medium-sized, three-story brick building in the heart of Flint, making it accessible to kids all over town. It started small, in a Cape Cod house, and had recently expanded once the community caught wind of what it offered — tutoring, sports teams, African dance, theater, and counseling amongst the other activities put on every month. The goal was to keep kids off the street and provide them with a safe, free, fun environment away from home.

Fab got Breeon a blanket and some food before placing an emergency call to her cousin Gayle, one of the owners of

The Center, who also acted as the counselor. Fab and Gayle, along with their cousins Dee, Mike, and Ari, had opened it in their community to help kids when they found themselves in situations like this or worse.

Once she sent a group text and informed her cousins on what was going on, she grabbed a first aid kit and joined Breeon in the main room. She didn't want to pressure the young girl to tell her what happened, but she had to know. Legally she had an obligation to the kids who came to the community center, and even if she didn't, she loved them all like they were her own. Seeing Breeon like this was hard for her.

"How long were you sitting outside?" Fab asked softly, handing Breeon a towel to put on her face.

"Almost two hours."

"You shouldn't be sitting out here by yourself. We post our numbers on the door. Why didn't you call somebody? Where's Leah?"

Breeon shrugged her shoulders at the mention of her best friend. Usually, that would be the first person she called if they weren't already joined at the hip, but there was so much going on she didn't even know if they were friends anymore. Tears slid down her face as she wept softly. Fab rubbed her back to comfort her.

"Breeon, tell me what happened."

The young girl took a deep breath and prepared to share details of what had been happening with her. She had been keeping a secret from everyone she knew, even Leah, but

THE CENTER: BREEON'S STORY

now, Breeon had to get help because she would never be able to fix it on her own.

Waiting patiently, Fab racked her brain, trying to figure out what could have possibly happened. Breeon was a regular at The Center and seemed to always be happy and in good spirits. She was a beautiful, well-behaved honor student who had close relationships with family and friends. Some teens frequented The Center who caused Fab and her cousins to worry about them on a regular, but Breeon wasn't one of them.

It took her a minute, but Breeon finally figured out where to begin her story. She didn't know what would happen to the people involved, and at this point, she didn't care. Telling someone what was going on was necessary, and she hadn't sat on the stairs for two hours for nothing. Swallowing hard and taking a deep breath, Breeon started the story at the exact point her problems began.

Two

"So, are you gonna tell me?"

I dragged my feet as I walked alongside my best friend Leah, pondering on whether or not I would answer her question. It was early on a Saturday afternoon, and we were walking to her boyfriend Will's house. Usually, I would be up and ready to go, but on this day, I would have still been in bed watching reruns of *Insecure* if Leah's annoying ass hadn't shown up at my door.

"I don't really wanna talk about it," I admitted, even though I knew that would never be an acceptable answer. Best friends didn't roll like that, and we had been just that since kindergarten.

"I ain't talkin' to Jay no more. He ain't breaking up with his girlfriend, just like you said."

Jay was a guy I had met a few months ago at a football game. He was a senior, a few years older than me, and had gotten my number. Jay called and texted every day all day for months before confessing he already had a girlfriend. He kept swearing he would break up with her, then last night finally told me he wasn't going to do it. I hated admitting Leah had been right, but she was, and I knew she only had my best interest at heart.

Leah shook her head with an angry look on her face. Anytime someone hurt me, she took it personal, and I could tell by the look on her face, the only thing on her crazy mind was getting revenge, not saying she was right. That's why I loved her.

"I never liked his ass anyway. You deserve better."

I nodded my head. I knew she was right, but when the hell was better gonna come? It seemed like I'd been single forever, while she had been in a committed relationship for over a year.

"Why didn't you have Will come get us?" I complained more than questioned.

"Because I wanted us to have this time to talk about Jay."

There was an awkward moment of silence.

"You know… Brice still asks about you," she said, referring to Brice Foster, her boyfriend William Moore's best friend.

"Girl, I ain't about to even entertain that."

"Why not?"

"Because he already has too many girls. They be fightin'

over him and stuff."

I shook my head.

"I think he really likes you," she sang.

I rolled my eyes as we continued to walk. I knew I would more than likely be seeing Brice at Will's house, which was probably why she had mentioned his crush on me. Truthfully, I liked Brice and all, but I knew I could never really date him. The part about girls fighting over him was true, but I also knew he was having sex... and a lot of it. That was something I just wasn't doing yet. I was probably the last damn virgin in the state of Michigan, but I didn't care. I wanted to wait until I was with somebody that I knew truly loved me. Brice struck me as the type of guy that would only want to get into my pants.

"Well, forget all that. Let's talk about homecoming!" Leah exclaimed, nudging me and doing her best to cheer me up.

The summer was winding down, and school would start again soon. Leah and I would be sophomores this year, and therefore no longer be the lowest in the pecking order. Not only that, but Leah was also dating Will. He would be a junior and was already one of the most popular boys in school, which meant we were let into the unspoken upperclassmen club, which automatically made us cool. We were also thinking about trying out for varsity cheerleading. I had a feeling this year would be so much fun, so Leah bringing up homecoming lifted my spirits a little. It was the most anticipated time of the school year.

We made predictions about spirit week and the colors we

planned to wear to the dance as we approached Will's house. He and Brice shared a small two-bedroom house a few blocks away from school, which I thought was a lie until I saw it for myself. His mother was a successful real estate agent, and his father traveled a lot for the security company he owned. She had gotten him a house at the beginning of the summer because she planned to travel more with his father and said it was closer to school, and his grandmother's house. I had heard Leah make the comment that they had done it to further push him from their life, but she never really told me what she meant by that.

Leah knocked on the door, and in just a few seconds, Will was there with a smile on his face.

We had all known each other since Kindergarten, but Will had disappeared for a few years while his father opened another business. He came back in our fourth-grade year and his fifth, and it was like he never left. Now, he had grown out of the buck teethed little boy he was. Those years of braces had done him good because now he had the straightest, whitest teeth I had ever seen, which only complimented his big brown eyes and cinnamon-colored skin. He was one of the few boys in school that already had facial hair, which he kept in a neatly shaven goatee. Will and Leah started going together during our eighth-grade year. At first, it was weird, but after a while, it became regular.

"Hey baby," he said to Leah, kissing her on the lips. She smiled and kissed him again.

I rolled my eyes. Will and Leah's affection didn't bother me any other time, but this time it was only reminding me I was single as hell and would once again be the third wheel.

Will noticed my sour face and tried to imitate it.

"What's up, Bree? Why the long face?"

I shook my head and waved my hand like it was no big deal.

"I'm cool. I just got some stuff goin' on."

"Well, it'll be okay." He gave me a hug, which was very much needed.

I walked in, and Brice, Will's best friend and roommate, was sitting on the couch. Brice Foster was also a junior at Brindle Crest High School and popular by association because of Will. Smooth, chocolate skin covered his slim, muscular frame. He had height, about 5'10, but he wasn't as tall as Will, who was well over six feet. Brice had light brown eyes that drove all the girls crazy and a head full of soft, silky curls.

"Aw shit here come the fashion models," he joked, referring to Leah and I dressed to the T as if we were going somewhere special. I had on a pink and white sundress, and Leah was wearing a purple romper.

Ever since we were small, Leah had been obsessed with her appearance. She was the type of little girl that would cry if her outfit got dirty or wrinkled until someone changed her clothes. Somewhere along the way, she influenced me to be the same, and we never left the house unless our hair, makeup, and outfits were perfect. Brice sat up on the couch, so there was enough room for us to sit down. Leah sat on the loveseat next to Will, which left the seat open for me to sit with Brice, who was smiling like a kid who had just gotten

THE CENTER: BREEON'S STORY

into the cookie jar.

"What y'all in here doin'?" Leah asked, settling under Will's arm, which he had wrapped around her as soon as they sat down.

"Shit, in here bored. He dont wanna play the game no more cuz he tired of gettin' beat, so we were thinking about going to The Center to hoop."

"That sounds fun. It's always something goin' on at The Center. I always go there when I'm bored."

"Well, we out then," Will said, hopping up. Let me go throw some clothes on."

He grabbed Leah's hand and pulled her off the couch, and she gave me a sneaky smile. I immediately got my phone out of my purse to keep myself entertained in the meantime. After checking all of my social media sites to see if I had any notifications, I scrolled through YouTube, trying to find something interesting to watch.

"Wanna watch something?" Brice asked, holding out the remote. I shrugged my shoulders and went to grab it. He took hold of my hand and pulled me on his lap.

"Brice, what are you doin'?" I asked, attempting to get up, but he held me down.

"I'll let you up if you tell me why you won't give me a chance." I rolled my eyes.

"Brice, you ask me this every time you see me."

"And you never give me a real answer."

"Brice, you got too many girls. They get in fights and stuff over you, and you know that ain't what I'm about."

"That's cuz I'm single. I'm tryna make you mine so I can drop all them girls. You know they don't hold a candle to you."

I can't lie. He was giving me butterflies, and it felt good, especially after finding out I wasn't good enough for Jay. Maybe I could give him a chance. Who's to say it would be all bad? Brice was best friends with Will, and I was like his little sister. Maybe that alone would give him good reason not to play me.

"Just give me a chance," he whispered in my ear, "I want you to be mine."

My body shivered, and I hoped he didn't feel it. I knew what Brice was doing, and I had to stay strong. Dudes like him were always smooth talkers, which is how he had been able to finesse so many girls. What made me so different?

"I know you don't trust me, and you shouldn't. Give me a chance, and I promise I'll make you happy."

Brice's breath was warm against my ear and neck, and I unwillingly closed my eyes. I felt his warm lips on my neck, but I didn't move like I usually would. It felt so good.

"Please. Give me a chance?"

This time I nodded my head, and he kissed my neck again.

"I'mma make you so happy, you'll see."

THE CENTER: BREEON'S STORY

"Yeah, we will see," I said, although I didn't know if he had even heard it because it was below a whisper.

We sat together and let the Food Network channel play through our awkward silence.

"Ooohhh looks like I see a love connection," Leah roared, announcing her arrival.

I jumped up off of Brice's lap like she was my mother, and I had been caught with a boy in my room. She had a sly smile on her face.

"Y'all ready? Will asked, coming out of the room. He noticed the looks on our faces.

"What's wrong with y'all?"

"I don't know, baby... but Breeon will tell me all about it!"

***

The plan was to go to The Center so the boys could play basketball, but instead, we stumbled into a Kick it Session. It was an event they held randomly three times a month. They usually tried to do it when there were a large amount of people there, and they would order pizzas and get snacks. Everyone gathered in the common room, which had couches, bean bags, and floor mats to talk about any and everything under the sun. For now, the topic was consent.

"I'm not saying consent ain't important," a boy named Curtis said, "but how do I know if she's not consentin' if she's not sayin' nothin'?"

"That's a good question," Miss Ari said, talking over the few people who were responding. She was another owner of The Center and was what we called our Success Guru.

Her overall responsibility was planning college trips, and introducing us to information about skilled trade jobs, but she did so much more. Ari was the person that made sure we had whatever we needed to succeed in whatever we were doing. If you were writing a book, she would find information on how to publish one. If she knew you were an actress, she made sure to get information about opportunities available in the area and would make sure you had the transportation to get there. She even organized an early breakfast on the days we had big tests so that we wouldn't go to school on an empty stomach. Kick it Sessions was also something she started along with Mr. Mike.

"What would be a reason somebody who does not consent to whatever is going on won't say anything?" Miss Ari asked.

"Scared," Jillian said.

"Or maybe she feels like because she told him she is going to, or they are almost there that it's too late to say she doesn't want to," Hannah said.

"Those are both two reasons, but y'all know that doesn't matter, right?"

Her response was met with a mixed chorus of different answers, and she put her hand up to bring the volume in the room back down so everyone could hear her.

"Listen to me carefully, y'all. Remember, it does not

matter how far y'all have gone. You can always say no. I don't care if y'all of completely naked and in the bed. If you decide you don't want to do it and you say no, he has to stop… period."

"Yeah, but it ain't always girls!" a boy named Chamberlain yelled from the back of the room. "Girls don't be caring about consent either, but because they are girls, people don't talk about that."

A few of the guys laughed at him and called him some names, but Miss Ari immediately put a stop to it.

"Hey! None of that in here or y'all can go," she scolded, making eye contact with the guys who were causing the issue. "Chamberlain is absolutely right. Men can be violated or abused, just like a woman can. It just isn't talked about as much because a lot of men are too ashamed to come forward to say it is happening. They are afraid to get negative reactions from people," Miss Ari finished, eyeballing the guys again.

Mr. Mike had been silent for a while, just listening to what everyone was saying. He was a mentor for the boys and always used Kick it Sessions to get an idea of what was really going on in their heads.

"It's a lot of stuff you need to pay attention to when dealing with somebody on that level. But y'all know it's okay to ask the person if they are okay, or if they like the direction things are going. If you notice their body language changes, ask why. Assuming it's okay can get you in a lot of trouble when all you have to do is simply ask and make sure," he said.

D. RENEA

***

We hung around The Center after the kick it session until Miss Fab, and Miss Ari put us out like they always had to. We would probably stay the night there if they let us, but they only had lock-ins once or twice a year because they said it took them three weeks to recuperate.

Breeon and I went back to Will's house, deciding to make the most of the hour we had left for curfew. Instead of going inside, we sat outside, playing music and taking pictures and videos for our social media sites.

"Breeon, come here," Brice said. He was seated on a lawn chair on the porch.

When I went over to him, he pulled me in his lap once again, the camera on his phone ready to take a selfie.

"Unt-uh, what are you doing?" I asked, covering my face with my hand.

"I want you to take a picture with me and let everybody know we off the market."

"Off the market? I'm not off the market yet."

"Well, you will be soon," he said and took the picture before I had a chance to protest. "Got it."

"No, let me see," I said, trying to take the phone from him. He waved his arms around to keep me from getting the phone.

"Nope, gone. You gonna try to delete it."

"No, I ain't! Just let me see."

THE CENTER: BREEON'S STORY

He held the phone to my face without allowing me to touch it. I had to admit, the picture was cute, and we made a good couple. That didn't mean I was off the market though. I didn't care what Brice said.

Leah and I stayed at Will's house as long as we could before he dropped us off at home. Leah stayed around the corner from me with her mom, but she was at my house more than she was at her own. My father, Patrick Bennett, had been there for Leah, whose father refused to be in her life.

"Brice and Breeon sitting in a tree! K.I.S.S.I.N.G!" Leah sang as I unlocked the front door. The lady's voice on the alarm system announced that the front door was open.

"Oh, shut up!"

"Fa real, it's the cutest thing," she gushed as she followed me upstairs. "Now we can go on double dates and chill together. It's gonna be so fun!"

"Don't get ahead of yourself. We're just talking."

"Yeah, for now. You know you always had a little crush on Brice."

"He just better act right. I ain't like none of his other girls."

"Oh, I know. And I'll be around him too, so he won't be able to get away with nothing."

I sat on the bed and watched Snapchat videos and waited

for my turn in the shower. Once we had on our pajamas, we laid together in my queen-sized bed and talked, the way we ended every day. Leah had her own room at my house that daddy had painted pink years ago, but we always slept together except on the rare occasion we needed a break from each other.

"Girl, Kaycee texted me," Leah announced, referring to one of our close friends. Our circle was small and had been since fourth grade. Although we all had other people we associated with, everybody knew Leah, Kaycee, Tatiana, Raven, and I was always gonna rock together.

"What she say?"

"Nothing, trying to see what we were doing later this week. She wanna have a movie night, hollering about how we all need to hang before school starts," Leah said, putting her hair in a high ponytail.

She watched as I went through the tedious process of twisting my shoulder-length, thick brown hair into two-strand twists so it would be nice and curly the next day. It was times like this I missed having relaxers or wished I had hair like Leah.

"That sounds fun! I'm down. When she tryna do it?"

"I don't know. Let me text her," Leah said, already unlocking her phone.

We chatted about Brice and Will, as well as the plans we had for the rest of the summer before we both drifted off to sleep much earlier than expected and without even watching our favorite reality TV show, which was watching us

THE CENTER: BREEON'S STORY

instead.

***

My phone blared and woke me out of my sleep. Leah, who slept hard, was dead to the world and didn't stir at all. Refusing to look at the bright screen, I answered, unsure of who was calling so late.

"Hello?"

"Damn, fa real Breeon? That's what you doin'?"

"What? Who is this?" I asked, annoyed and confused.

"Man, it's Jay. You know who it is."

"What's going on? What are you talking about?" I whispered, not wanting to wake Leah.

"You don't waste no time moving on from me, huh? You already got you a new dude."

"What?"

"I saw homeboy's little Instagram post claiming you. You just had dudes sittin' waiting, huh?"

"Why do you even care? Don't you got a girl?"

"I knew you were gonna throw that shit in my face, man."

"Throw what in your face? The truth?"

"Man, fuck all that! You know how I feel about you."

"Jay, you can't keep playing games with me, you got a

whole ass girlfriend!"

Jay said nothing, but I could hear him breathing. The nerve of this dude! Here he was with a girlfriend, but thinking he was gonna dictate my life and who I was with… I think not!

"Bye, Jay. Don't call me anymore. Be happy with your girl, that's what you wanted."

I didn't wait for a response because what more could he say? When he called back, I ignored it, then started getting notifications for text messages. I knew it was him, so instead of reading them, I put my phone on silent, turned over, and returned to my deep slumber.

***

Once I started to get to know Brice on a personal level, falling for him was surprisingly easy. He immediately wanted to spend as much time as he could with me and would call and text me when we weren't together. Brice said it was his way of letting me know not only that he was thinking about me but also to prove to me he wasn't entertaining any other girls. He knew I didn't trust him when it came to that, so I appreciated him making the effort.

Chilling at Brice's house was like an everyday routine now. Leah and I got up, got dressed, and Brice or Will would pick us up and take us to their house. This time, Will had picked us up, and when we walked in, Brice was sitting on the couch. I smiled when I saw him, but he didn't look as happy to see me. I sat next to him, and Leah followed Will upstairs.

THE CENTER: BREEON'S STORY

"What's wrong?" I asked, noticing the displeased look on his face.

"What you got on?" he asked, irritated.

I looked down at the jean shorts and crop top I was wearing before I smartly responded, "Clothes."

"I don't want you dressing like that. That's showing too much."

I shook my head. This time I was the one confused.

"Have you been outside today? It's almost 80 degrees, and it's not even noon."

"I just don't want my girl showing off everything that's supposed to be mine."

"I'm not showing off anything. You can't see anything."

"I can see your ass cheeks hanging out the back. You know what dudes say about girls that dress like that?"

I didn't really know what to say. I couldn't argue with whatever Brice was saying dudes said about the way I dressed because I wasn't a guy. What I knew was there was nothing wrong with what I had on. My daddy had seen it before I left the house!

"I'm gonna wear what I wanna wear, Brice. You not my daddy."

Brice nodded his head, and I could tell he was pissed.

"So, it's cool for me to compromise to make you happy, but you can't do the same for me?"

"How is this the same thing?"

"Because I'm going above and beyond to prove to you that you can trust me, and all I'm doing is asking you to change the way you dress a little, tryna get you to respect yourself, and it's a problem. The fuck is that about?"

"So now I don't respect myself? You didn't have a problem with the way I dressed before, telling me how different I was."

"You wasn't my woman before, now you are."

"Am I?" I asked, more to make him angry than anything.

"Fuck it. I guess not."

Brice got up from the couch and left me sitting there like a fool. Maybe I was being unreasonable. He was compromising with me and doing his best to prove I could be the man he wanted, so maybe I needed to do the same. After a few minutes, I went inside Brice's room and sat on his bed.

After a little while, Leah and Will were still in his room, and I was lying on the bed in Brice's. He was up putting away some clothes he had recently washed, and I just watched. Once he was finished, Brice crawled in bed with me, laying his head on my chest. Immediately he started planting small kisses on my neck, which caused chills all up and down my spine. He softly kissed my lips and slid his tongue inside. I moaned softly, wrapping my arms around his neck.

Brice's hands traveled down my body, sliding down my

exposed belly and stopping to unbutton my shorts. Immediately my body tensed.

"Stop," I said, grabbing his hands.

"What's wrong?" he asked, kissing my neck. "You don't like it?"

"Yeah… I do."

"So why I gotta stop?"

"Because I don't want to… I never did it before."

He stopped and looked me in the eyes. Brice was so close our noses were touching.

"So, you are a virgin?" he asked like he was confirming what he'd heard was true.

I nodded my head and looked away. I don't know why talking about being a virgin always made me feel a little ashamed. Maybe because everybody was doing it, and I felt like I was missing out on something. Either way, I knew how special being a virgin was, so I wasn't about to just have sex with anybody.

"It's cool," he said, kissing me on the lips. "I'm not gonna force you or nothing. I wouldn't do anything like that to you."

Brice then smiled, and so did I. He wasn't the first guy that I had turned down, but sometimes the reaction wasn't as nice as that.

We lay in his bed for a while just talking until Will and

Leah barged in so we could go get food. Brice held my hand and opened all the doors for me. He treated me like I was special, totally different from how I had seen him be with other girls. Maybe he did think I was special, and since he thought that, maybe dressing a little more like he wanted to wasn't that big of a deal.

THE CENTER: BREEON'S STORY

Three

"Brienna Enriquez… George Evans…"

Weeks had passed, and we had finally come upon the first day of school, which meant freedom was over. Mr. Dawson was standing in front of the class, taking attendance. You could tell none of us were ready for school to start because the energy was on zero. Some kids had their heads on their desks, obviously not used to waking up that early. Others were like zombies, just staring out into space, probably asleep with their eyes open.

We attended Brindle Crest High School, which was considered one of the nicer schools in the area. It was a large, two-story glass building with a football and tennis field. Kids from all over town attended, making it a diverse environment. Brindle students were all different races and nationalities, and they came from so many different walks of life. It was one of the reasons my daddy moved into the district.

"Breeon Bennett."

I raised my hand, giving a nonverbal announcement of my presence. He nodded and smiled.

After attendance, we sat in class for about another fifteen minutes before the bell rang, signaling it was time for the next hour. Saying nothing, we got out of our seats and headed to our next classes.

The energy in the hallway was a little livelier. Loud greetings and conversations could be heard about beaches, swimming pools, late-night parties, and every other thing a teenager could get into when they didn't have the pressures of school lingering over their heads.

I made my way down the hallway, smiling when I saw Raven approaching me. She had spent the entire summer with her aunt in Louisiana, so this was my first time seeing her since a few weeks after school had got out.

"Bree!! Hey, boo!" she exclaimed, wrapping her arms around me. "OMG! We have so much to talk about, girl! I mean, I know we texted and stuff over the summer, but there was just some stuff I had to wait until I saw you to tell you!"

I hugged her back and laughed.

Raven was the prettiest and craziest girl in our group. First of all, she had a shape that I would kill for! Her hips were wide, her waist was small, and she had the perfect size breasts to compliment it all. Although she ate the most out of all of us, her stomach stayed flat, and all her weight seemed to go to her booty, which all the boys loved. Her skin was a mahogany brown, and her mother was a natural hair stylist, so her hair had been in dreadlocks since we were in grade school. They now hung down the middle of her back. All of this was complemented by big dark brown eyes, a button nose, and full lips.

"What happened? I'm sure the dudes were giving you all the love down south!"

"Girl, they were, and they were fine as hell too! I mean, dark chocolate guys just like I like 'em!" she squealed in delight. "Where is your next class?"

"Upstairs. It's math with Miss Winters. I don't know who the hell put me in a math class first thing in the morning, but they need to be slapped!"

I hated having my tough classes first thing in the morning. It really sucked when there was a quiz. At least if it was toward the end of the day, I could study in my other classes, or ask around to find out what was on it. Having to take an exam first hour was like being a crash test dummy. You didn't know what the outcome would be, and everyone would look at you for the results.

"I feel you. My class is up there too. We should meet at the same place every day and walk together."

"Cool."

As we walked to class, Raven went on and on about a boy she told me she'd met while visiting her aunt named Jeff. She had told me all about him on the phone but hadn't told me they'd had sex before she left. She swore he was the best lover she ever had. It was weird being one of the few ones in my group of friends that hadn't had sex yet, but I tried not to let that pressure me. Sure I wondered what it was like and all that, but I wasn't about to just *do it* to just anybody to find out.

Nearing my classroom, we ran into Man-Man. His actual name was Fredrick Jones, but he hated it and always insisted on being called what his family called him. Even the teachers called him Man-Man, and he was well known because he wasn't the most well-behaved kid in school.

"Aw shit, look at the crew piecing itself back together again. I knew it wouldn't take long!" he yelled from all the way down the hall.

Raven and I both laughed as we approached him. He stretched out his arms, and we wrapped ours around him at the same time, making one big group hug in the middle of the hallway.

"Where the rest of the clique at?"

"They here somewhere."

"Um-hum, I'll find them later. Y'all know my brother is moving back home for a while, so when he does, don't be tryna kick me to the curb like y'all don't know me."

"Man-Man, you know that is *exactly* what we gonna do!" Raven said, then immediately hugged him and told him she was joking.

Man-Man's brother Frank was just a couple of years older than us. We all used to think he was so fine until we realized he looked at us all like little sisters.

THE CENTER: BREEON'S STORY

"Yeah, it's alright. He the cool one, but I'm better looking."

Raven and I both gave each other a look and burst out laughing, which intensified Man-Man's fake jealous act.

We chatted for as long as we could before the warning bell rang. I made it to my class just in time and sat right in the middle. Although I was good at math, I didn't care much for it, which meant this hour was gonna go by extremely slow.

***

The day went by pretty fast for the first day, especially for my schedule. After math class, I had physical science with Mrs. Waters, then US History with Mr. Andrews, and finally, I got a break at lunch. It turns out I only had lunch with Tatiana and Kaycee. We had gotten lucky last year, and somehow, we'd all gotten the same lunch, but that wasn't the case this time. So, the three of us grabbed a table by the window before we got our food.

"These freshmen are irritating the hell outta me already," Kaycee complained, sitting down at the table.

"Like we weren't freshmen last year," Tati said, laughing.

Kaycee and Tatiana had come along in middle school and became inseparable with Leah, Raven, and I immediately. Kaycee was the quiet one out of the group, but she was really smart. She took all honors classes, was a member of The National Honor Society, president of the Thespian Club, and made the honor roll every semester. She was the tallest of us all, standing at 5'9" and had dark chocolate skin. Her brown hair was usually braided or hidden by a sew-in. Today it was fresh box braids that looked as if they had been done on the way to school.

Tatiana was the comedian of the group. No matter the situation, she could find the humor, and that was always needed. She was also a great listener and was the one I usually went to when I wanted level-headed advice. Tati was a thick girl and was proud of it, always advocating for big girls and how they were just as pretty and healthy as skinny ones. She had long, blonde hair, green eyes, and freckles all over her face that only enhanced her beauty. Her lips were pink and full, putting to rest the myth that white people had small lips.

"Yeah, we were freshmen last year but was weren't loud, obnoxious, irritating, ugly, and in the way."

"*Daaamn Kaycee.* Did you have to go in on them like that? Why they gotta be ugly?"

"I don't know. They just are," she said, laughing and finally taking a bite of her burger. "And I told that lady no damn Mayonnaise!" She tossed the burger to the side and put her head in her hands dramatically. "This is going to be a bad year!"

Kaycee's acting skills were kicking in, and we all rolled our eyes.

"So, how is the first day going for y'all?" I asked.

"Boring as usual," Tatiana said. "I hate the first day of school."

"I don't. It's the only day we get to sit and do nothing. Enjoy it. It won't happen again until next year."

"Then we'll be upperclassmen, officially anyway," Kaycee said, referring to the fact that we always hung with an older crowd because of Leah.

"And one step closer to graduation! I can't wait to get the hell up outta here!" Kaycee exclaimed.

"Of course you can't, you've been applying for college since we were in the sixth grade," Tati said. Kaycee laughed while sticking up her middle finger.

"Whatever Tati. Breeon, your boo don't got this lunch?"

"No, he has last lunch."

"That's my worse fear," Tati said, holding her chest. "Getting last lunch. Do you know how hungry I'd be in fourth hour?"

"You are greedy," Kaycee said.

"Yup, I gotta eat every hour on the hour."

We continued to chat and eat our lunch until the bell rang. After throwing away our trash, we parted ways, and I headed upstairs to art class. As I was ascending the stairs, Brice was descending and made sure he was walking right into me.

"There goes my baby," he said in his best Usher impression. Wrapping his arms around me, he pulled me into the corner and out of the way of traffic.

"I missed you. You coming over after school?"

"Probably, but you know my daddy is gonna start cracking down now that school is back in."

"Then I better get all my time in now," Brice said, pulling me close again and kissing my neck before one of the hall monitors walked by and told us to break it up. "Meet me at the parking lot door right after school."

"Okay," I said, freeing myself of his muscular arm and heading upstairs as the tardy bell rang.

I made it to art class just as Mr. Gordon was closing the door. At least I could look forward to an easy class after lunch.

* * *

"So how was your summer? Did you take any trips?" Miss Stone, a Civics teacher, asked. She was my absolute favorite teacher of all time, and I usually stopped by her class and talked to her at least two or three times a week.

"I went to visit my family in Texas with my dad, but other than that, I just stayed around this boring town."

"And how is your mother?"

Miss Stone was one of the few people I allowed to ask me about my mother, but even when she did, I got a knot in my throat. I hated talking about her.

"I haven't seen her in months," I mumbled.

"Hey, that's her loss, not yours. Don't you let that worry you. Is your dad okay?"

THE CENTER: BREEON'S STORY

"Yup. Patrolling the streets, same as always."

"He knows you dating Brice Foster yet?"

I looked at her, eyes wide in disbelief.

"Who told you?"

"Teachers are the eyes and ears of the school. Nothing happens without us knowing, no matter how y'all try to hide it. Just be careful with him, Bree."

"I will. Shoot, speaking of Brice, I was supposed to meet him right after school!" I said, jumping off of the desk I had been sitting on and grabbing my bookbag. "I'll see you tomorrow Miss Stone!"

"See you then!"

I ran out of the room and bumped right into Man-Man.

"Damn, where you rushing off to, Bree? You almost knocked me over."

"Yeah, right," I said, laughing at his exaggeration. "I'm going to meet Brice."

"So, you really are dating him, huh? I always thought you were all about the books. I never saw you falling for a playboy like Brice."

"He is not a playboy... well, at least not no more."

"If you say so."

I ignored his last comment and continued toward the parking lot exit with Man-Man on my heels since he was headed the same way. Brice was standing at the door, waiting with his keys in his hand, and as soon as he saw me, I could tell he was annoyed. Stalking over, he grabbed my arm.

"Where the hell you been? I've been looking for you. I asked Leah where you were, and she didn't even know," Brice spoke loud enough to get everybody's attention, and I'm sure the embarrassment could be seen all over my face.

"I was talking to Miss Stone," I tried to explain, but Brice wasn't trying to hear none of that. Still holding my arm, he dragged me to his car, and I reluctantly got inside.

"The hell was you doin' wit Man-Man?"

"I wasn't with him!" I snapped. "He was walking the same way as me when I left Miss Stone's class."

Brice shook his head.

"I don't like that shit. You switchin' yo ass all in front of him while I'm standing at the door, waiting like a fool. You think I'm stupid?" Brice's eyes narrowed as he glared at me.

I put on my seatbelt as he sped out of the parking lot. Rubber burned as he turned on the main road and headed toward his house.

"You can just take me home," I said over the music he was playing. Brice had a lot of nerve making a scene like that and thinking I would still come chill with him.

"What?"

"Take me home."

THE CENTER: BREEON'S STORY

"Why, so you can go call your boy Man-Man?"

"Yeah, maybe so—"

Before I could say another word, Brice reached over and pushed me in my chest. It wasn't a *punch*, because his hand wasn't in a fist, but it was enough force to take my breath away.

"You keep playing games with me, Breeon. Keep playing games."

My mouth was still open in shock as I tried to gather what had just happened. Had Brice really just put his hands on me?

"Take. Me. Home," I slowly said, letting Brice know I meant it.

He sped up a little more and made it to my house in record time. When I got out of the car, Brice sped off again before I could even close the door and left me standing in the driveway, not even making sure I made it safely inside.

***

"How was the first day of school, baby?" my dad asked when he came in from work.

He still had on his blue uniform, complete with the gun, badge and black boots. This was the reason most guys had been scared to date me. Not only was he a cop, but he was also tall, standing at almost 6'2". He had dark chocolate skin, his black hair was cut into a low fade, and his arms were nearly the size of my head from his rigorous workout regimen.

"It was good. I got all my hard classes in the morning."

"That's good, get it all out the way."

"I think the opposite, but I'll try to look at it that way. How was work?"

"Tiring," he said, coming into my room and sitting at my vanity chair. "You cook?"

I nodded my head.

"Chicken and rice. I put your plate in the microwave."

"My baby," he said with a big smile. "Your momma ain't been by, has she?"

I shook my head while resisting the urge to roll my eyes

"Okay," he said, trying to hide the look of disappointment on his face before walking out of the room.

As hard as my daddy was, the only soft spot he had was for my mother and me. He loved her dirty drawers, and part of me hated him for it. Anytime she came by, he was begging her to stay. I had stopped doing that when I was five years old.

I listened as my dad fumbled around in the kitchen, warming up his food. The walls shook as he talked on the phone to his partner while finishing his meal. I adored my Daddy, and as much as I wanted to talk to him about the Brice situation, I knew what would come of it. Daddy had a gun and had told me since I was a young girl, he had no problem using it if any man ever disrespected me. I couldn't risk him doing something crazy and going to jail. Then I wouldn't have a dad either. So, since I technically wasn't supposed to be dating anyway, I kept the incident to myself.

* * *

I didn't hear from Brice until later that night. I was lying in bed watching another episode of *Love & Hip-Hop* (like I hadn't already seen it a million times) when my phone rang. When his name popped up on my screen, I looked at it for a long time before I answered it.

"Hello," I said dryly, making sure he knew I was still mad.

"Baby... can we talk?"

"We are talking."

"Look, I know I acted crazy after school—"

"Yeah, you acted crazy, and you embarrassed the hell outta me! Dragging me out of the school like you my daddy."

"I know, baby, I know. I am so sorry. I just let my mind get the best of me. I was waiting for you, and nobody knew where you were. Then you come down the hall, and I see Man-Man sniffing all around your ass. I just know how beautiful you are, and I don't want anybody else to have you."

"So, you don't trust me?"

"Yeah, I do. I don't trust him."

"It wasn't Man-Man that you were dragging out the school."

There was a moment of silence. I knew he had no response for that.

"I'm sorry, Breeon. I'll never do no shit like that again."

Now it was my turn to be silent. I knew it was wrong for Brice to put his hands on me, but it was kind of cute that he was so jealous. Brice was popular, and all the girls wanted him, so the fact that he was paying attention to me with so many other pretty girls walking around did make me feel kind of special, especially being only a sophomore. And while he was wrong for putting his hands on me, I was also wrong for saying what I said. Neither one of us was innocent. We just had to learn to communicate better and stop pushing each other's buttons.

THE CENTER: BREEON'S STORY

Four

"What color are you and Brice wearing to homecoming?" Raven asked as we sat on the couch at The Center, books in our laps.

It was a weekday, and we were there for an after school study session that was held twice a week. Everyone would come there to do their homework, and the kids who were better in certain subjects would help others. It was amazing how people's grades rose when The Center offered weekly study sessions. They provided snacks and even hired tutors when needed.

"We talked about red or orange. I don't really like the color orange though, so I'm probably gonna make him wear red. You got a date yet?"

"No, but I think I'm just gonna go with Terrance. He asked first, and he's fun, so I know I will have a good time."

"I like Terrance for you. Why don't y'all date?"

"Girl, because he fun, but he childish. I can't take him seriously."

"Y'all would be cute together."

"Whatever," Raven voiced, putting her book down and going to the other side of the room to the girl who was motioning for her to come help with a science question. Raven was a whiz at anything science.

I continued to work on my math questions. After a few minutes, Raven returned, and we continued to chat while doing our homework.

"Where is Leah? I thought she was coming to study session today?" Raven asked.

"You know Leah never comes to study sessions. She's probably somewhere laying up under Will as usual."

Raven laughed as Jay walked in carrying his bookbag. His eyes scanned the room before they landed on me. I tried to pretend I was focused on something in my math book as he made his way over to the couch.

"No he ain't about to bring his ass over here," Raven mumbled, trying her best not to move her lips.

"Wassup Raven, hey Breeon," he said.

"Hey," we replied in unison.

"Can I talk to you for a minute, Bree?"

I was just about to shake my head when Raven got up to help someone with another question, leaving the spot next to me wide open. Jay didn't waste any time sitting down.

"Long time no see," he said, opening his bookbag. He pulled out a Civics book and a notebook without ever taking his eyes off of me. "Miss you."

"Boy, please. You don't miss me. You miss having somebody around when your girl is busy."

"Is that really what you thought it was?"

"You weren't about to leave your girl Jay. You think I'm stupid?"

He smacked his lips and slid his hand down his face.

"You know I was falling for you. I ain't gon' lie. At first, that's what it was, but you got to me," he said, placing his hand over his heart.

I looked back down at my book, trying my best not to make eye contact.

"Why you leave me, though, Bree? Like… Damn, I told you not to give up on me and look at you. You Brice's girl now."

He shook his head, and I sort of shrugged my shoulders. He had to see how this was his fault. Reaching over to softly rub my arm, he looked at me longingly.

"Damn, I miss you," he whispered. "I miss your kisses."

"Stop," I said, pushing him away. "Do your homework."

He opened the book and pretended to focus until Raven came back and gave him the death stare for stealing her seat.

He gave it back to her and went to a sit at a nearby table.

"What did he want?"

"Girl, nothing. He's feeling like a fool because he thought I would wait for him forever."

* * *

After the study session, Miss Gayle took Raven and me home. She acted as the social worker at The Center and was the person people went to when they had problems and made sure everybody was safe in their home lives.

After getting inside and showering, I turned the Crock-Pot off that my father had left on and made myself a plate of the garlic chicken, carrots, and potatoes and poured myself a tall glass of iced tea. I got up to my bedroom where I'd left my phone on the charger, and I had three missed calls from Brice. I grabbed the phone to call him back, but he was calling again before I could.

"Hey baby—"

"Where you at?"

"What?"

"Where you at?"

"I'm at home. Why? What is wrong with you?"

"You ain't get that picture I sent you?"

"No, I was downstairs. Hold on."

I took the phone away from my ear, and sure enough, I

THE CENTER: BREEON'S STORY

had a missed text message from Brice. When I opened it, there was a picture he'd sent of Jay and I sitting on the couch at The Center. My heart sank because I could only imagine what kinds of ideas he had in his head.

"Brice, I don't know who sent you that picture or why, but ain't nothing happen. He just sat next to me."

"Nah, man, you tryna make a fool of me! First that shit at the school a few weeks ago with Man-Man, and now you all cuddled up with some dude? Ain't that the dude from Center High you was talking to before me?"

"Yeah, but he just came and sat next to me."

"It's funny. You did all this when I was tryna get with you, talking about me being a player and you the one playing me!"

"No, I'm not, Brice. I didn't do anything!"

"You know what, I'm bout to pull up on you. Come outside."

I didn't get to respond because he hung up in my face. My mood had changed entirely. The food that was once mouthwatering didn't even look appetizing, and my ice was melting in my tea. I didn't feel like dealing with Brice, but I knew if I didn't talk to him, he would definitely suspect something. So, after slipping on sweatpants and a t-shirt, I went outside where Brice was parked on the street in front of my house. He started going in on me as soon as I got in.

"Tell me what the fuck happened, Breeon," he scolded.

"Nothing happened, Brice, I told you. He just sat next to

me—"

"Look like y'all was talking in the picture. Y'all didn't talk?"

"I mean, we spoke, but that's it. I don't know why you gettin' all mad about this. I didn't do anything, and I don't appreciate people sending pictures of me to you trying to make something out of nothing."

"Nah, they just tryna let me know my girl out here being a hoe."

My mouth dropped open. A hoe? I was a virgin.

"Don't call me no hoe! I did nothing wrong, and I can't help who talks to me or where they sit."

"Yeah, but you can help who you talk to. I don't want you talkin' to him or Man-Man no more."

"What? I've known Man-Man since we were kids."

"I don't care. I bet not catch you talking to him, or this time it *will* be his ass I'm draggin'."

The last thing I wanted was to bring problems to anybody. Man-Man had done nothing, and neither did Jay, but Brice wasn't trying to hear that. He barely let me get a word in as he continued to yell at me. I sat there like a child hoping that he would tire himself out, and as I did, I started to think maybe us being in a relationship wasn't such a good idea. He didn't trust me, and we seemed to argue more than anything. I found myself walking on eggshells all the time, afraid I would do, say, or wear something that made him mad. I said nothing, though, and eventually, he let me get

THE CENTER: BREEON'S STORY

out and go back in the house.

* * *

"Oh my goodness, Leah, COME ON!" I said as I stood at the bathroom door, watching Leah apply mascara to her already beautiful eyelashes. It didn't matter what time she woke up. She always took forever to get ready because Leah refused to leave the house unless she looked flawless. It didn't matter where she was going.

Today we were going to the movies with Brice and Will, so I could understand why she wanted to look good, but I had been standing at that door for ten minutes. Besides, Leah was a flawless beauty. Her light brown skin was like butter. She had long, silky black hair, and her big hazel eyes and full lips complimented it all. Leah was perfect and looked like a movie star as soon as she rolled out of bed in the morning. Deep down inside, sometimes I felt ugly being next to her. It wasn't her fault. She was just beautiful effortlessly.

"I'm almost done, Breeon, damn. You act like they outside or something," she said, spinning around in the mirror so she could look at her body in the white jeans and pink and white bodysuit she was wearing. Her hair was pulled into a ponytail at the top of her head, and silver hoops hung out of her ears. After applying more lip gloss, she finally turned off the light.

"Okay, I'm ready. Can I take my makeup case to my room?" she asked sarcastically.

"You've taken this long, might as well."

After taking an abundance of selfies and posting them on social media, we sat on the porch and waited for the boys.

"So, how are things going with you and Brice?"

I shrugged my shoulders.

"I honestly don't know. He be trippin' sometimes."

"Trippin' how?"

"Just getting' real mad about every little thing. One day Man-Man was walking behind me, and he went crazy, talkin' about I was flirtin' or something."

"Were you?"

"Please, girl. We talkin' about *Man-Man*. Nobody likes Man-Man. He's... Man-Man."

Leah laughed.

"Yeah, I was about to be worried."

"I don't know. I just don't like how mad Brice gets over everything."

"He hasn't hit you, has he?" She glared at me.

"No."

Technically I wasn't lying. He hadn't hit me. It was a push. Besides, I didn't want to tell anybody because they would make it a big deal and it really wasn't that.

"Well, don't pay that no attention. You fine, smart, and got a bomb ass personality. He probably just scared to lose you. Will did the same thing last year when I danced with Trayvell at Sadies, remember?"

"Yeah, but you and Will had gotten into an argument that night, and you and Trayvell used to talk. You were trying to make Will jealous, so that was a little different."

She let out a sneaky laugh and put her finger over her lips as if someone was around to hear us.

"As long as he doesn't hit you, don't worry about it. Brice ain't used to being in relationships, so he probably doesn't trust easy. Once he sees how loyal you are, he won't act like that no more."

That's why I loved Leah. She made everything make so much sense.

Will and Brice pulled up a few minutes later. Brice got out of the front seat and left the door open for Leah. As soon as he saw me, he smiled so sweetly I almost forgot about our argument.

"Hey, you," Brice greeted, wrapping me in his arms. I gave him a half-hearted hug back.

"Come on, baby, let's have a good day," he said like I'd been the one who was mad at him. Brice's change in mood was weird sometimes.

Brice opened the door and climbed in after me, grabbing my hand and kissing it. After putting on her seatbelt, Leah turned around and gave him a look that would kill from the front seat.

"You better stop being mean to my best friend," she said.

"I fight boys too."

Brice let out a chuckle but looked at me like he was uncomfortable. I ignored that and looked out the window as the car pulled off.

* * *

At the movies, we got our tickets, and Will and Brice got in line to get the snacks while I accompanied Leah to the bathroom. Once we were out, they were waiting for us. We found seats in the middle of the theater and waited for the movie to begin. Jordan Peele had just released a new horror movie, and we knew the theater would be packed, so we had gotten there a little early. Nothing was playing on the screen yet, except those random videos and trivia questions that they display before the previews start.

"What was Leah talking about in the car?" Brice questioned, handing me the bucket of popcorn.

"Oh, I had just told her about something you got mad at me about, that's all."

He said nothing for a minute. Brice just chewed the popcorn, and looked at the screen like he was deep in thought.

"What did you tell her?"

"About that incident with Man-Man," I admitted. "She can even tell you I ain't thinking about that boy."

"Why would you tell her that?"

"Why not?"

"Because that's our business."

"But Leah is my best friend. I tell her everything."

"And I'm your man. What I want don't matter?"

Now I was uncomfortable. Was Brice asking me to keep secrets from Leah? That was something I had never done, so it wouldn't even feel right. And why did our relationship need to be so secretive?

"It does matter, but—"

"Then you should listen to what I say. If I tell you I don't want you talking to somebody about *our* business, that should just be what it is. I'm tryna be in a relationship with *you*. Not Leah, Raven, Tatiana, or Kaycee… just you."

I didn't say anything even though I wanted to. I wanted to remind Brice again that he wasn't my daddy, and I could talk to whoever I wanted. That I could tell my friends whatever I wanted, and I didn't need his permission to do it, but we had been having such a great day so far, and I didn't want to ruin it over something stupid. Besides, our fighting would only ruin Will and Leah's date too. So, I just nodded my head instead of debating or arguing.

"Okay, Brice. From now on, our business is our business."

Five

Believe it or not, after the Jay incident, things between Brice and I got a lot better. He didn't seem to trip out as much about little stuff, although he did still have a problem with the way I dressed. To make him happy, I started FaceTiming him in the morning so he could help me pick out my outfit. It made things a lot better because then he already knew what I was wearing and therefore couldn't complain or accuse me of trying to get attention.

We spent every second we could together, and if we were not together, we were on the phone or texting. It felt good to have somebody and not be the third wheel how I used to be. I enjoyed being with Brice, but I missed my girls, so when Tatiana finally put together a movie night at her house, I was thrilled to spend some time with them.

Leah and I were the first to arrive. My dad dropped us off in his squad car at the three-bedroom bungalow Kaycee lived in with her grandparents. Her mother had passed away when she was little, and her father couldn't raise her on his own.

She swung the door open with a bright smile.

"Hey, y'all! Y'all got dropped off by the law, huh?" Tati quizzed, waving at my daddy. He smiled and waved back before cruising away.

"You know daddy drive that car more than he drives his own. I just hope he keeps that same energy when I get my license."

We laughed as she led us into the family room. Kaycee had gone all out for us. She had fruit, chips and dip, everybody's favorite candy, Rotel and Doritos, along with a nice big pitcher of Kool-Aid since hers was the best in the world. Kaycee loved putting on events and decorating and usually tried to do something for each one of our birthdays. This must have been a make-up celebration for Tatiana since her birthday was over the summer.

"What movies are we watching?"

"That depends. Are we in the mood for scary, funny, or sad?"

Leah and I both voted for scary but decided to wait for everyone to arrive to make the decision. We made our plates, and before long, Raven and Tati had shown up. The majority voted on a comedy, so Kaycee put in *Friday*, a classic movie that never gets old. Just as we were getting under the covers and starting the movie, a text came to my phone from Brice.

Brice: *WYD?*

Me: *At Kaycee's house watching movies with my girls. Wyd?*

After a few minutes, he replied.

Brice: *I wanna see you. Can you sneak away?*

Me: *No…the movie just started.*

My phone buzzed again before I even had a chance to put it down.

Brice: *Damn. Friends come before me again, huh?*

I immediately rolled my eyes. Brice couldn't be serious. Lately, I had been spending more time with him than anyone, including Leah. Didn't he understand that I needed time with just my friends? Why was he taking it so personally?

Me: *Idk what you talking about. I haven't spent time with my friends since school started back. I be with you every day.*

Brice: *For all I know, it's probably some dudes over there too.*

Me: *It's not. Her grandparents don't even allow boys in the house.*

Brice: *Take a picture and send it to me.*

Brice was ruining what had started as a perfect movie night. Here we all were lounging around the living room in comfy clothes, head scarfs, and blankets, and he really wanted me to take a picture just to prove to him there were no boys here? I could understand him not being trustworthy, but he had to learn to start believing me.

THE CENTER: BREEON'S STORY

Me: *I'm not sending you a picture. I told you there weren't any boys here!*

"Damn Breeon, you can't take your eyes away from the phone for two seconds," Tati said, slapping me in the head with a pillow. "But you be the first one talking about us."

"Right," Kaycee agreed. "We know you love your boo, but it's our time now."

She was right. I was a huge advocate for putting phones away and spending time, and here I was, unable to stop texting Brice. I couldn't understand why he seemed to get jealous anytime I spent time with somebody else, but he had to get over it. So, instead of reading his reply, I put my phone on vibrate and put it on the table with everybody else's.

* * *

I tried my best to enjoy the movie, but it was damn near impossible since my phone kept vibrating nonstop throughout the entire movie. I knew it was Brice, and reading the messages would only get me upset, so I just continued to ignore them. By the time Craig and Smokey got shot at, I had fifteen missed calls and almost thirty unread text messages. My heart was in my stomach because I knew he was mad.

Tati's grandmother took us home, and I was quiet the whole ride. My sophomore year was not going at all as I'd planned. I wanted it to be filled with good grades, football games, dances, and carefree fun with my girls. The fact that I had a boyfriend was supposed to be the icing on the cake, but it was beginning to feel like just the opposite. I was so focused on making him happy my grades were slipping, and anything I did that didn't involve him became an argument. For so long, I'd wanted a relationship, but I didn't know it would be like this.

We pulled up at my house first, and I got out. Leah had decided to go home to check on her mom, which was probably a good thing because I had a feeling Brice and I was about to have a huge blowup. Before I could get in the house and return his calls, though, he was already calling me back.

Before I could even say hello, I could hear Brice yelling.

"You know what? Fuck you, Bree! Do whatever it is you do. I knew I was wasting my time wit' you! Don't you know I can have any girl I want?"

I didn't say a word. For almost five minutes, I sat on the phone and allowed Brice to yell at me, disrespect me, and degrade me for simply not answering my phone during a movie. The things he was saying to me were hurtful, and I'd had enough.

"You know what, Brice?" I yelled over him. "I'm done! I don't wanna do this anymore!"

"What?" he asked, clearly shocked by what I'd said but unable to bring his adrenaline down.

"You heard me. I don't wanna be with you no more. I'm not about to keep letting you disrespect me for no reason! I did nothing wrong!"

Brice started to yell something, but I just hung up the

THE CENTER: BREEON'S STORY

phone. Immediately the calls and texts started, but I blocked his number before he had a chance to upset me any more than he already had.

Six

"Alright, everybody, settle down. You still got at least ten more minutes before the bell rings."

Mrs. Anderson was trying her best to yell over us, but all of our voices were collectively making one loud class. It was the end of the day, and we were all ready to go. Fed up, she stood behind her desk and put her hands around her mouth.

"Everybody, sit down and shut up!"

Immediately, the class got quiet, and everyone slid in their seats. Mrs. Anderson was one of the coolest teachers in the school, but making her yell was the last step before she unleashed her wrath, and if she did that, nobody was going home on time.

"Now, that's more like it. If I would've walked in from the hallway, I would've thought I was in the wrong room. Y'all know I don't play that loud mess."

THE CENTER: BREEON'S STORY

Mrs. Anderson was sitting back down as her classroom door swung open. My mouth dropped open when I saw Brice standing there with a huge teddy bear, chocolates, and flowers. It had been almost a week since I'd broken up with him. He'd been blocked ever since, and I'd had been avoiding him at school.

"Well, to what do we owe the pleasure of this visit, Mr. Foster?" Mrs. Anderson asked. She had been teaching at that school for a million years, so she knew all the kids by name (even if they weren't her students) and whether or not their siblings attended previously.

"I wanted to see if it was okay if I talked to Breeon for a minute."

Mrs. Anderson looked at me with a sweet smile on her face.

"Breeon," she sang, "you can go in the hallway if you want to."

My entire body was hot as I slid out of my seat. Maybe it was because everybody's eyes were staring a hole through me. It felt like it took forever for me to make it to the door, and when I did, Brice was looking down at me with a half-smile. I followed him into the hallway and closed the door so that we could have our privacy.

"What do you want, Brice?" I asked, crossing my arms over my chest. He may have impressed Mrs. Anderson with his little presentation, but I was not amused. I was embarrassed as hell!

"I came to bring you this," he said, shoving all the items

toward me "And I wanted to apologize for the way I acted. It was out of line. I shouldn't have disrespected you like that. I let my anger get the best of me."

I was opening my mouth to apologize before Brice continued talking and ruined it.

"You just can't be ignoring me like that, baby. I start thinking about stuff, and it makes me crazy."

I rolled my eyes and pushed the stuff back at him.

"You just can't accept responsibility for your actions, huh? You always gotta find a way to blame me. I told you I was watching a movie with my friends, so you knew where I was. You chose to act that way and say the things you said. You can't just apologize without putting the blame on somebody else?"

I turned to go back into class, but Brice grabbed my arm.

"Okay, okay, okay baby… I'm sorry. You right, and I'm sorry."

Brice took a deep breath.

"I know I'm a lot of work, and I get jealous a lot. I don't mean to be like that. It's just I'm used to people leaving me. My parents left me when I was a baby, and my foster family just collect their check. They don't care what happens to me. Then I got with you, and for the first time, I knew what it felt like to have somebody care for me, and losing you scares me."

My heart fluttered as Brice said those words. I had been dreaming of the day a guy would talk to me like this.

THE CENTER: BREEON'S STORY

"I love you, Breeon, and I don't wanna lose you. Can you please give me another chance?"

Everything in my body was telling me to say no. I didn't like the way being with Brice made me feel. I was always worried about doing something that would make him mad because it was never something I meant to do. It was like playing a game that I didn't know the rules to.

Brice could sense my hesitation because he grabbed my hand, intertwining our fingers.

"Please baby. I love you."

Before I even knew it, I was nodding my head, and Brice had dropped all the stuff and pulled me into a hug.

"I'm fa real...I love you, Bree. I promise you won't regret this decision."

***

"Man, I still cannot believe you took all that to her class!" Leah exclaimed, laughing for the tenth time that day.

It was a few weeks later, and Leah, Will, Brice and I were gathered in the living room at their house. We all looked as she had herself a good, knee-slapping laugh.

"What is so funny about that?" Will asked. Leah sat up and looked at him like he had lost his mind.

"Breeon is probably the shyest person in the world. Everybody knows she does not like to be the center of attention. I'm surprised she didn't slap the hell outta you."

Brice wrapped his arm around me, kissing me on the side

of my head.

"I was ready to do anything to get my baby back. If that hadn't worked, I would've just tried something else."

I blushed, this time kissing him. Ever since he had brought that stuff to my class, Brice had been treating me like a queen. I was finally feeling happy and in love, and the feeling was so good I never wanted it to go away.

"OMG, get a room!" Leah exclaimed, laughing. I gave her a 'I know you ain't talking' look, and we both laughed.

Will flipped through every single channel on his TV before finally settling on watching some movie with a lot of sex and shooting. This must have been turning Brice on because he couldn't keep his hands off of me. I laughed, nervously moving his hands from where they were traveling. True, I was falling for Brice, but I wasn't ready to have sex just yet.

We sat on the couch and watched TV for a few hours before we got up and headed to The Center. The boys were going to basketball practice with Coach Dee. There weren't many community centers in the area, but when Coach found some, he organized games for us. Most of the time, it was basketball and football, but every now and then, he would get us into a track meet or tennis game.

While they were playing basketball, we went inside to do some African dancing with Fab. She had classes for an hour three times a week, although it usually ran longer. Leah and I had been coming every week for a couple of years now, and the benefits it was having on my body was tremendous. Not only was I gaining strength and muscles in places I'd never had, but I was also getting in better shape too. Before I'd started dancing, I could barely run up and down my stairs without losing my breath.

When we descended the stairs to the basement where dance classes were held, we could already hear the drums. We quickly dropped our purses and took off our shoes and socks before joining Miss Fab and four other girls on the floor where they were warming up. We followed her lead as she started warm-ups, and I swear I was already sweating before we even started practicing.

Once we were finally finished almost an hour later, we sat on the floor talking and catching our breaths.

"Are y'all all ready for homecoming next week?" Miss Fab asked, handing us all bottles of water.

The response was a small chorus of excited yes, unsure, I guess, and a couple of shoulder shrugs.

"What colors y'all wearing?" she asked.

We all responded one at a time. Since Leah and I would be attending Will and Brice's junior prom this year, they let us pick the colors. Will and Leah would be wearing yellow and silver, and Brice and I were wearing red and gold. Hannah, Queta, Shareena, and Frances told us what colors they were wearing, and we continued talking homecoming plans until we heard the boys' footsteps coming in from where they had been on the basketball court. We all gathered upstairs and joined the boys in the common area.

"How was practice?" I asked, sitting next to Brice.

"It went good. Leah just needs to tell her boy to quit hoggin' the ball."

Will cut his eyes at Brice.

"Nah Breeon, tell your boy to get open, and I will, actin' like he doesn't know how to play offense. I'm tellin' you now, don't bring that shit to the school games."

"Alright, alright, leave it on the court!" Coach Dee yelled.

He was standing by the basement door, talking to Miss Fab still holding the basketball under his arm. His whistle was around his neck as it always was, and his light brown calves seemed to glisten in the sun shining through the window. I used to have the biggest crush on Coach Dee and would imagine being left alone at The Center with him. I wasn't as obsessed now, but he was still nice to look at.

"Breeon!" Brice said, snapping his fingers in my face.

"Yeah?"

"You ready to go?" he quizzed, following my gaze to see what I was looking at. When he looked back at me, I could tell he'd figured it out.

"Yeah," I said, grabbing his hand before he had a chance to say anything.

Brice looked at Coach Dee again, and I could see his jawbone twitch. He said nothing, though. He just stood, pulled me out of my seat, and followed me out the door.

THE CENTER: BREEON'S STORY

Seven

"Aww, look at my beautiful baby!" daddy exclaimed from behind his iPhone screen.

He was snapping so many pictures of me that I was afraid he would never let us leave. Even though the phone was blocking most of his face, I could see that prideful smile, and at that moment, I truly felt like I was the most beautiful girl in the world. It didn't matter that it wasn't true, as long as my Daddy thought so.

"Daddy," I groaned, giggling, "we gotta go. We're already late, and we're supposed to meet Will and Leah at the door."

"Okay, okay. Just a few more."

I smiled again, as Brice wrapped his arms around my waist. I didn't remember my dad being this anxious when I'd gone to homecoming last year, and I couldn't decide if it was because this time I had a date, or that my red, lace-up-back mermaid dress was fitting my curves perfectly. Either way, it seemed like my daddy did not want to let me leave the house.

"Daddy, fa real," I said after he'd moved us by the tree in my front yard. He was really getting his photography on, and I could tell Brice was starting to get annoyed. "We really gotta go."

"Okay, okay, okay, I'm done."

Dad pulled me into a hug and gave me a soft kiss on my forehead so he wouldn't mess up my makeup.

"You look so beautiful, baby, just like your momma. I know she would be so happy if she were here."

I sighed and bowed my head. He was talking to me like she was dead. If my mother wanted to be there, she absolutely could have been. Obviously, she had important things going on in her life, and being my mother wasn't one of them. I would not ruin my special moment with my dad telling him that, though. He knew what it was.

"Thank you, daddy. I love you."

"I love you too, baby," he expressed, smiling at me before directing his attention to Brice.

"You be careful with my daughter, young man," he declared, giving him a firm handshake. "I want you to understand that you have my *very* precious cargo in your possession tonight... drive and act accordingly."

"Understood, sir. I will."

My dad nodded his head and followed us to the car. Brice opened the door for me, and when I got in, as soon as Brice's back was turned, my Father started inaudibly reminding me to put my seatbelt on by putting on his imaginary one and mouthing 'seat belt' over and over. His years as a cop had made him paranoid. I was just glad he didn't embarrass me.

He stood on the porch watching as we drove off and I watched him in the mirror until he was out of sight. It was a relief to be from under his watchful eye. The whole time I was afraid Brice would do or say something to me and make my father uncomfortable and end my night before it even started. I was glad he had been the perfect gentleman.

"Sorry about that," I said, apologizing for my father causing us to be late. "He does that sometimes."

"It's cool. You do look beautiful," Brice voiced, looking at me out the corner of his eye. "I never see you wear makeup. It looks real good on you."

"Thank you," I said, blushing.

Secretly, I hated makeup, but Miss Fab was the only one who could do it and make it look good on me. She believed makeup was supposed to complement your features, so she applied it accordingly. She was always available at The Center on the day of homecoming, prom, or any major event to do hair and makeup for the girls. It had started as a way to just help a few girls in need, but now none of us wanted anyone but her doing it, so she was usually booked all day. You had to talk fast to get an appointment with her. I was glad Leah and I had secured ours.

THE CENTER: BREEON'S STORY

Brice continued complimenting me as we pulled up to the school. Opening my door again, he grabbed my hand and led me to the entrance of the school where Leah and Will were waiting.

"Well, it's about time. I love you, but if it started raining, I was about to go in," Leah complained as soon as she saw me.

That didn't stop her from hugging me and telling me how good I looked. I returned the compliment. She looked flawless in her open-back silver sequin dress, and it made me wonder what she would wear to prom to top it. Her long hair was pulled to the side in a mermaid braid, and silver jewelry accented her ears, neck, and wrist.

Joining hands with our dates, we entered the building, and we could already hear the music flooding from the gym. An edited version of Cardi B's "Bodak Yellow" was blasting, and Leah and I almost lost our minds. She was a die-hard Cardi fan, but I liked both Cardi and Nicki. I didn't understand why there needed to be a competition when they both were dope. I wasn't much of a rap fan anyway. Jhene Aiko was my favorite.

We ran into the gym and ignored the chaperones as we started grinding on Will and Brice to the music. We stood face-to-face, dancing with them and each other at the same time.

We pretty much stayed that way for another four or five songs before we decided to take pictures before we sweated away all of Miss Fab's hard work. When we returned to the gym Leah and I went to find our girls while Will and Brice found their group of homeboys sitting at a table toward the back of the gym.

"Well, it's about time we found y'all!" Tati said, extending her arms and hugging us both.

She had on a navy blue, V-neck chiffon dress that hugged every one of her curves just like she liked. Her hair was flat ironed into a cute bob. Raven was nearby talking to Man-Man and drinking punch. She had on a floral print ball gown, and her dreads were pulled into a high ponytail. She smiled and waved at us. Kaycee had decided to sit this dance out.

"This DJ is playin' all the good shit, girl! I'm pleasantly surprised," Tati said over the music.

"That's the same thing Breeon and I was saying! I hope they keep this DJ for all future dances!"

We chatted for a minute before another hit blasted through the speakers, and we ran to the dance floor. Raven grabbed Man-Man's hand, and he joined us. The four of us surrounded him on the dance floor, and he had a look on his face like he was the man. Sooner or later, Brice cut in, and I started dancing with him while my girls continued grinding on Man-Man.

* * *

The dance went extremely fast, probably because we were having so much fun! We danced all night, and although Brice stayed on top of me, it was still fun. Over time, I was hoping we could have a relationship like Will and Leah. They hardly ever got jealous of each other, and

THE CENTER: BREEON'S STORY

both let the other have fun and dance with other people. Will didn't even say anything when Leah danced with Malachi, and everybody knew Malachi had the biggest crush on Leah. Will didn't care. In the end, she was his girl, and a three-minute dance would not change that.

After the dance, we had dinner at Sagano's before returning to Brice and Will's place. It was nearing nine o'clock by then, and I had to be home by eleven. I knew my Daddy would be waiting at the door with his gun on his hip. He'd already called me three times to check on me. As soon as we got into the house, Will chased Leah upstairs, already eager to rip her pretty dress off of her body. I took off my shoes and collapsed on the couch. Brice came and sat next to me, pulling my feet on his lap to massage them.

"I don't know how y'all girls walk around all day in shoes like that," he said, examining the indentations the straps of my shoes had made.

"Beauty is pain," I said, recalling when Leah had said it to me when she taught me to walk in heels when we were twelve. "You get used to it."

Brice raised my feet to his lips and kissed them tenderly. I watched with wide eyes as he made a trail of kissed from my foot to my ankle... to my calf... to my knee... I knew where this was going. It was weird because I wanted to, but I was terrified.

"Brice," I said, grabbing his hands. "You know I-I'm—"

"I know baby, I know. But you know I love you, right?" he whispered, kissing my neck. My eyes closed in pleasure.

"Yes. I love you too."

"Don't be scared, baby. I never wanna hurt you. I will never hurt you."

I nodded my head, and in that moment, I had forgotten all about the other incidents — the losing his temper, pushing me... all of it. It's weird how hard it is to see the bad when everything is going good. Brice had been perfect for months, and if that was any indication of how it would always be, I knew I was making the right decision.

Brice grabbed my hand and helped me up off of the couch before leading me to his bedroom. My feet felt like weights as I followed, my heart beating so loudly in my chest that I was sure there was still music playing somewhere. When I entered his bedroom, I took a deep breath because I knew when I came back out, I would be leaving something behind that I would never get back.

Eight

"You should've seen her, baby. She looked so pretty."

It was the middle of the night, and I had awoken out of my sleep to go to the bathroom. I could hear my father talking, and based on his voice, I knew it was to my mother.

"She does," I heard her reply, obviously looking at a picture of me on his phone. "She looks so beautiful."

"Baby, she needs you," he said, and I could feel my blood start to boil.

I didn't need her, and I wished he would stop telling her that lie. I needed her when it was my first day of elementary school... when I had my first crush... when I started my period. Now, no, I didn't need her. Not at all.

"I know Pat, I know."

I crept down the hallway toward their bedroom and put my ear up to the door so I could hear them better.

"So why don't you just come home. Just stay here with us. Whatever you need me to do, I'll do, baby, I promise. Just don't leave again."

I hated hearing my daddy beg. I understood how much he loved her, and that broke my heart — more than anything, I wanted my father to move on. Lord only knows what I would give to stumble into his room in the middle of the night and see him with another woman. Unlike other teens, I would actually be happy! I knew that would never happen, though. He would hold on to her until the end.

"I want to Pat, I do. I just- I can't see her right now."

By *her*, she meant me. It had probably been years since I heard her say my name. I wondered if she even knew it anymore.

"We can be a family, Trice, a happy family. All I ever wanted to do was make you happy."

I shook my head. My dad was still in denial. My mother wasn't staying away because she was on drugs, or had some kind of addiction. She had a husband and family in another town. After a six-month-long affair with my dad, she got pregnant with me. She had planned to pin me on her husband, but he found out about her affair almost halfway through her pregnancy. It was too late to have an abortion so, after giving birth to me, she dropped me off to my father and went back home to her husband and other kids. I used to feel sad knowing that while I was crying myself to sleep at night for my mom, she was across town kissing and tucking her other kids into bed. She didn't understand how her coming around affected my dad and me, and for that

THE CENTER: BREEON'S STORY

reason, I just wished she would go away and stay away.

"Patrick, I don't wanna hurt you or her."

There was that word again. *Her.* Like I was someone that didn't deserve to be acknowledged. I was a constant reminder of her betrayal to the man she truly loved…a walking and talking mistake.

"Then, just stay here. We can be enough for you. I can be enough for you."

I could hear them start to kiss, and I got sick to my stomach. I hated my mother so much, and sometimes I hated my father for loving her. I crept to the bathroom, then back into my room and bed before I heard something else I didn't want to witness.

* * *

"Did she say your name this time?" Leah asked as we lay on her bed, our homework out in front of us.

I was multitasking — talking to Leah, doing my homework, and texting Brice all at the same time. Leah, on the other hand, was only scrolling through Instagram, ignoring the blank US History worksheets in front of her. Just as I suspected, my mother was gone by the time the sun was up, and I'd come to Leah's after school to avoid any awkward discussion about her with my father.

"Nope. You know she barely acknowledges me," I said, shrugging my shoulders like I didn't care, but it hurt like hell. That was hard to admit, even to my best friend.

"Well fuck her, that's her loss."

"How many other kids you think she got?"

Leah just glared at me, a look of pity on her face.

"I don't know, boo, but they have nothing to do with you. She is the one that is missing out."

What she was saying sounded good just like it did every time Leah tried to reassure me my mother's absence was not a reflection of me. It didn't stop me from thinking about it, though. If I were prettier, like Leah, she probably would want me.

"It doesn't matter anyway," I said after a brief moment of pretending I was focusing on my homework. "As far as I'm concerned, I don't have a momma, and I don't need one."

Leah nodded her head, and we moved on from the topic.

It had been months since homecoming, and it was cold outside. Midterms were just around the corner, and while I was gathering all my information to begin studying, Leah couldn't care less. We had been doing homework for almost an hour, and she didn't have one word on her paper.

"Okay, come on, let's finish this homework so we can be free for the rest of the night.

Leah nodded her head, laughing at some video she was watching but making no attempt to focus on the work. She stayed that way for the next half hour as I finished up mine. By the time I was done, she had gotten on the phone with Will and had completely abandoned her papers and gone into the bathroom. I was hoping coming over and doing my homework would motivate her. Unfortunately, nothing seemed to help. Leah just didn't care about her grades. I didn't sweat her about it, though, or make her feel bad because I knew the things she went through in her home life. Instead, I closed my papers in my book and put it in my bookbag. Sliding her books and papers in front of me, I started on her homework. She wasn't about to fail, not on my watch.

* * *

Weeks went by, and my mother's visit was still bothering me. I tried to ignore it, but it was evident in almost every aspect of my life. I was moody, lazy, tired, and I couldn't focus on anything for a long period of time. It didn't help that our science teacher had assigned us to a class project, and I'd been paired with Jeffrey Bonds, and he wasn't exactly a hard worker. We made plans to meet right after school to get started.

"I hope you're ready to work because I'm telling you now, I'm not about to do everything," I announced as soon as I made it to where he was waiting for me at the table. His goofy ass already had a smile on his face.

"Here you go, already talking mess. You can't even give me a chance to prove myself."

"You have had a few years to prove yourself, Jeff. We've had classes together before."

He rolled his eyes and laugh, sticking the earbud back into one of his ears. I could hear Kendrick Lamar rapping from where I was seated across from him.

"You gonna turn that off?"

"I need my music to work."

"Whatever."

We spent about an hour together in the library, splitting the responsibilities for the project. After we had our tasks, we planned to meet again in a couple of days with the work we completed so we could start putting everything together. After threatening Jeff a few more times, we went our separate ways.

I pulled my cell phone out of my bookbag to call Brice, but it was dead. Things had been going better with us for the most part, and I was constantly making sure it stayed that way. I knew that he would be angry that I had not been answering my phone. It couldn't have been because I had stayed after school. Leah was supposed to tell him.

I waited on the bench in front of the school until Leah pulled up. Her mother's boyfriend Brandon hadn't had the car in a few weeks, and when she was in a good mood (or drunk enough), Leah could convince her Mom to let her drive it. When she pulled up, I hopped in.

"Hey, girl!" she greeted with an enormous smile.

"Hey, did you tell Brice I was staying after school to work on a project?" I asked as I got into the car.

"Oh shit, I forgot! I was rushing out after school."

I rolled my eyes.

"Damn Leah! I asked you right before school got

dismissed. You could've texted and told Will to tell him."

"I just said I forgot Breeon, damn what is the big damn deal? It ain't like y'all had plans or something."

"That's not the point. He likes to know where I am."

"Breeon, he was just with you a little while ago. I'm gonna tell him to calm the hell down."

"No, don't say anything to him," I urged, sounding a little more afraid than I meant to. She shot daggers at me with her eyes.

"What's up Breeon, what's the problem? Is Brice acting okay?"

"He's fine," I said with a slight attitude. "I just don't wanna make him mad."

"You didn't do anything, though."

"I know, I just... Don't say anything to him."

"Whatever," Leah quipped. She was dropping the issue for now, but I knew it wasn't the end of it. We rode in silence until we pulled up to my house.

"I'm sorry Breeon, I really didn't mean to forget."

"I know, it's okay. Sorry I was trippin'."

We smiled at each other. That's how our relationship was. Our fights never lasted more than a few minutes, and when Leah wrapped her arms around me and told me she loved me before I got out, I knew she meant it.

D. RENEA

THE CENTER: BREEON'S STORY

Nine

"Can y'all just tell me what's going on?" I asked from the backseat of the car.

Leah was driving, Kaycee was in the passenger seat, Tati was sitting next to me, and we were on our way to Raven's house. Apparently, they had something to talk to me about, but nobody wanted to tell me until we were all together. The only thing that annoyed me was they didn't wait until we were all together to announce they had news. The suspense was killing me.

"We will as soon as we get to Raven," Leah said, looking at me out the rearview mirror.

I rolled my eyes and kept my attitude until we pulled into Diamond Square Apartments, where Raven lived with her parents. As soon as we got to the door, she opened it with a smile.

"Hey y'all, come on in."

We followed her into her room and sat on the floor. Raven didn't like anyone sitting on her bed, especially with their clothes on. After we were all seated in a circle, I was the first one to break the silence.

"Y'all wanna tell me what the hell is going on?"

They all looked at each other, probably trying to decide who would break the news to me.

"Okay, Breeon," Raven spoke up. "I'll tell you since I was the one that got the information."

"What information?" I asked, not liking the feeling of being left out.

"Okay, so my friend goes to Pointe South, and she knows a girl that goes there named Gabrielle. She said that Gabrielle told her that she has been talking to Brice for months now," she voiced, referring to Pointe South High School, a private school in the suburbs.

"Talking like what?"

"*Talking*. Like dating. She said they had sex too."

The food in my stomach started to churn, and I could feel my blood getting hot.

"She's probably wrong. It might not be him."

"We thought that's what you would say, so we got screenshots," Leah said, holding her phone up to my face.

The number was definitely Brice's, and he was definitely talking to this girl like they were dating. To say I was mad was an understatement. As much as Brice was always on me about talking to other boys and being around them, I couldn't believe he was the one that had been being unfaithful!

"I'm sorry Breeon," Kaycee said. "I know how much you love Brice, but I gotta be honest... I don't like the way he treats you."

"Me either," Raven agreed. "He acts like he owns you or something. He wants to know where you are every second of the day."

Tatiana had been silent but was nodding her head in agreement.

"You know Brice is my boy," Leah said. Her relationship with him was different because he was her boyfriend's best friend. "But he do be trippin'. And as much as I like him, I love you, and I don't ever wanna see you hurt. Brice has always been a player, and I guess nothing will change."

I was listening to what they were saying, but my mind was on betrayal. I wanted them to finish this "intervention" so I could confront Brice about what I was being told.

When they were finally done, I had Leah send me the screenshots and take me to Will and Brice's house. When I got there, he was in his bedroom, and I went inside without even bothering to knock.

"Hey baby, I didn't know you were coming by," Brice greeted, getting up from his gaming chair to hug me. I pushed him away.

"We need to talk," I said, throwing my purse on his bed. "And we can start the conversation with you telling me who the fuck Gabrielle is."

Brice had a forced and confused look on his face.

"I don't know nobody named Gabrielle, baby."

"Right," I said, going into my phone and pulling up the screenshots. "So, this ain't your number?"

Brice looked at the phone for a long time, probably trying to come up with a lie to tell. He could save it, though, because the things he was saying in the messages made it obvious he knew exactly who Gabrielle was.

"Baby, I don't know that girl like that."

"You know what Brice, you trip on me all day, every day, every time I even speak to a dude, but you think this is okay?"

"So, you don't believe me?"

"*Believe you*?! Ain't this your phone number?"

"So, you gonna believe what your little friends tell you? You know they wanna break us up, right?" He asked, completely ignoring my question.

I had to laugh.

"You don't admit anything you do wrong. You always find a way to blame someone else."

"Okay, okay. I did text her Breeon, but that's it."

"So, you didn't have sex with her?"

He shook his head.

"No."

"Well, I don't care. This kind of stuff is not okay," I said, holding my phone up in his face. "I told you before I wasn't about to deal with you messing with other girls, and I'm not!"

"So, what you sayin'?" he asked.

"Just what it sounds like. I'm done with this relationship."

"Damn just like that? I don't even get a chance?"

"A chance to what? Break my heart? Hurt me? Nah, I'm straight."

I reached for the doorknob to leave the room, but he grabbed my arm and yanked me to him.

"Wait, don't leave, Breeon. Let's just talk about this."

"I don't wanna talk to you!" I yelled, trying to pull away from him. Brice wouldn't allow it, though. He just wrapped his arms around me, putting me into a forceful hug.

"Let go of me!"

"NO! Just talk to me, why you gotta leave?"

"Because I am done with you! You a no-good ass dude, just like I thought at first—"

Brice let me go and pushed me onto the bed. Before I had a chance to get up, he climbed on top of me, pinning my hands up over my head.

"You think you can just leave me for some bullshit?"

"Get off of me!"

"Nah, fuck that! You talkin' bout leaving me, I ain't lettin' you go."

I kicked with all of my strength as tears of frustration streamed from my eyes, but my 120 pounds was nothing compared to Brice's 210-pound weight. He was solid muscle too.

"Listen to me, Breeon. I love *you*. Gabrielle dont mean shit to me."

Just when I knew I wasn't going anywhere, the door swung open, and Will and Leah barged in.

"Aye, man, what the hell?" Will yelled, pulling Brice off of me. "The hell you doin.?"

Leah ran over to me and pulled me off of the bed.

"Breeon, you okay?" she asked, pulling me into her and cradling me like a child. "What the hell is goin' on?"

Will had pulled Brice out of the room to calm him down. I could still hear him yelling from the living room as if I'd done something wrong.

"Can you just take me home?" I asked, trying to keep my voice from shaking.

THE CENTER: BREEON'S STORY

"Yeah, of course," Leah answered without a second thought.

Grabbing my hand, she led me into Will's room where she put on the rest of her clothes. When we walked past the living room, I could feel Brice looking at me, but I refused to make eye contact.

"Breeon—" Brice started.

"Just leave her alone, man," Will said, shaking his head.

I was on Leah's heels getting out of that house, and she was moving just as fast. We hopped in the car, and she took off like she was the one trying to get away. As soon as we were down the street, she started going in.

"See, this is what we were talking about, Breeon. Brice be acting crazy, but I ain't ever seen him do no shit like that before!"

I was wiping my tears with a napkin I found in the glove compartment.

"You need to stay away from him, Breeon. He ain't right."

"I know."

She continued to lecture me the entire ride home, and when we pulled up, and I saw my Daddy's squad car in the driveway, I was hysterical.

"Aw man, my daddy's home!" I yelled, more tears gushing from my eyes. "If he sees me, he's gonna know something is wrong. I look like I've been crying?"

Leah looked at me and nodded her head.

"Shit," I said, wiping my face frantically with the napkin, ignoring the white pieces that were falling onto my face. The last thing I wanted was for my dad to see me like this and start asking questions.

"It's okay, Bree. I'll go in with you and distract him, so he doesn't see you."

I nodded my head, and as soon as the door to my house opened, I ran straight to my room. I could hear my father coming from the kitchen, but Leah was there, as promised.

"Hey daddy," she said, and I knew she was giving him a big hug.

"Hey baby, you okay?"

"Yeah, I'm good."

"Where's Bree?"

"Oh, she went upstairs to take a nap. She wasn't feeling good today."

I waited for his response.

"Okay, I'll let her rest."

I sighed a breath of relief. Leah's feet started to ascend the stairs before I heard my dad's voice again.

"And Leah, you left your room a mess the last time you were here. Clean it up and don't let it happen again."

"Okay, sorry, daddy."

THE CENTER: BREEON'S STORY

By the time Leah joined me upstairs, I was in my panties and bra and crawling into bed. I was still feeling uneasy from the altercation with Brice, but I was glad to be in my bed and clear of my father.

"You okay?" Leah asked, standing over my bed with narrow eyes, her arms folded across her chest.

"Yeah, I'm good now."

She sat on the bed, never taking her eyes off of me.

"Breeon, has Brice ever did that before? Like, hit you or something?"

"No, he never hit me," I said, hesitantly.

"But," Leah urged.

"It was like a push... just a small one."

Leah shook her head.

"That's not okay, Breeon. He has no right to put his hands on you!"

"Shhh!" I said, looking over her shoulder at my half-open bedroom door. Leah never shut doors all the way.

"I'm sorry," she said in a much lower tone. "But Breeon, you know that's not okay. That's why you didn't tell me."

Looking away, I nodded my head. Leah always could see right through me.

"We don't keep secrets from each other, Breeon. You know that."

"I know. It was just embarrassing and... stupid. I don't know."

"Look, I get it. Some stuff is hard to tell, but you don't have to be embarrassed to tell me anything. You already know I'm never gonna judge you."

Again, I nodded my head. Never in our lives had Leah proved herself to be anything but a loyal, best friend. I couldn't believe I had kept a secret from her.

"Okay, well, you go ahead and lay down. I'mma clean my room before daddy whoops my ass then I'll make you some of that nasty tea you like to make you feel better!"

THE CENTER: BREEON'S STORY

Ten

Breaking up with Brice was definitely an adjustment. Not only had we gone from being together every day to me avoiding him altogether, but I no longer felt comfortable hanging at Will's house. With it being one of mine and Leah's favorite hangouts, she now had to split her time between Will and me.

Time wasn't the only thing that had to change. Until our breakup, I didn't realize how much Brice controlled my decision making. It was weird being able to pick out my own clothes again or go where I wanted without checking in, but it was a welcome change. I felt free, and slowly but surely, my life was going back to what it had been before my relationship with Brice.

It didn't take him long at all to start trying to get me back. A few days after our fight, he started calling me and leaving voicemails. They started sweet with him apologizing repeatedly. Then, when he realized I wasn't responding, he started getting angry. Then the threats and belittling started. Once I realized he was up to his old tricks, I blocked him.

I succeeded in avoiding him for about a week or two before he finally caught up with me. I was walking home from the store one afternoon after school, and as soon as I turned on my street, I saw his car in my driveway. Immediately my body tensed, and I contemplated turning around just to avoid him, but I refused to run away from my own home. I would just walk past him like I didn't see him.

"Breeon, can I holla at you for a second?" Brice asked, getting up from the porch as soon as he saw me approaching.

"For what? I heard everything you needed to say in all them damn voicemails—"

"I know, I'm sorry about that—"

"You're sorry about everything, Brice."

For a minute, he said nothing. I could feel him staring at me as I put my key in the lock.

"I know what I did was wrong, and you have every right to never wanna see me again, but the reality is, my best friend and your best friend go together. I live with Will. Whether or not we like it, we're gonna see each other. It's better for everybody if we get along."

He was right. The last thing I wanted was to bring tension to Leah and Will's relationship because of us.

"Let me just take you to get some tea and talk to you."

THE CENTER: BREEON'S STORY

Again everything was telling me not to go, but just because our relationship had ended didn't mean I didn't love him. Maybe he did deserve a chance to explain himself, but I didn't feel comfortable being around him.

"No, Brice, just stay away from me."

"Breeon, please," he said, his voice shaking like he was on the brink of tears. "I'm so sorry."

By now, the door was opened, and my hand was on the knob. I should've just turned it and went inside, and that is exactly what I would have done if he hadn't said the next thing.

"Please don't just leave me like this baby. If you do, I'll kill myself. I don't even wanna live without you."

That did it for me. I didn't want anybody doing anything to hurt themselves because of me, and Brice had already had a suicide attempt in middle school when his biological mother died. I loved the hell out of Brice, and even though he hurt me, I didn't want him to die.

"Okay," I said, turning around and closing the door, "but we stay here."

He nodded his head and wiped his eyes with his sleeve. I followed him to the car, and we got inside to get out of the cold, but I didn't allow him to start the engine.

Brice smiled nervously, still not saying anything. He looked like he was trying to find the words to say to me on the dashboard of his car.

"Breeon, there ain't no excuse for the way I acted that

day at Will's house. I was trippin'. I disrespected you for absolutely no reason other than I got caught up. I am also sorry for talking to you like that and putting my hands on you. Like fa real, I've been fucked up ever since."

My body started feeling warm all over. These were exactly the words I'd wanted Brice to say to me. For once, he was taking accountability and not blaming me for his actions, so maybe he was making progress.

"I never wanted to hurt you, so the fact that I scared you hurt me even more."

I could feel my eyes stinging from tears, but I didn't want to cry. Brice was my first love, and I never wanted to be afraid of him either.

"I wish we could just start over. If I could just get another chance to prove to you that I'm not like that, I would."

I didn't know what to say. I also wished we could go back to the beginning and change the events of our relationship, but we both knew that was impossible.

"Breeon, I ain't ever loved no girl the way I love you. Can you please just give me one more chance? I know you tired of this, I just wanna prove to you that I'm not the type of dude you think I am."

"I don't know Brice—"

"Please, Bree?"

Brice grabbed my hand, kissed it, and looked into my eyes.

THE CENTER: BREEON'S STORY

"I don't know how this is gonna work, Brice. My friends don't like you, and Leah saw what happened, so she's never gonna get over it."

"They will. We just have to keep it between us for a while."

"What you mean? Why?" I asked, taken aback.

"Relationships are supposed to be between two people. When more people get involved, that's when shit gets complicated. Since we already have people against us, we need to take our time and try this again. Then when I prove to you how happy I can make you, you won't have a problem with what other people think about us."

Again, I was hesitant. Leah and I had just talked about keeping secrets from each other, and here I was contemplating doing it again. On the one hand, I didn't want to do it, but on the other hand, I felt it was necessary. Leah was already in a happy relationship, and I didn't want to be the third wheel to it my entire life. She didn't let me in on every aspect of her relationship with Will, so how was this any different?

What I didn't realize at the time was that I'd already been keeping secrets from everyone about Brice's temper and treatment of me. They based their opinion solely on their own observations and experiences. Brice was really good at convincing me I wasn't seeing what I was looking right at, so before I knew it, I was nodding my head and agreeing to his demands as if I'd been the one that messed up. He had my young head right where he wanted it, and I didn't even realize it.

D. RENEA

* * *

Juggling a secret relationship with Brice while trying to act normal with everyone else was a struggle, but the lying was the hardest part. Anytime we wanted to go on a date or spend time together, we had to lie and go somewhere we wouldn't be spotted. It felt wrong keeping a secret this big from my girls, but once I forgave Brice, I didn't want to hear any negative talk about him. My friends were not the type to keep their opinion to themselves and being torn between my friends, and my boyfriend was not on my high school bucket list.

As always, it didn't take long for things to get better between us. I quickly let my guard down and forgot all about the things he'd done. Being too forgiving had always been my downfall. However, the more time I spent with Brice, the more I felt like I'd made the right decision after all. He honestly was treating me like a queen, spending quality time with me, taking me on dates, and listening to my feelings. The altercation between us must have really messed him up because he hadn't even raised his voice at me since I'd given him another chance. My friends were wrong. Brice was nothing like they thought, and I was determined to prove that to them.

THE CENTER: BREEON'S STORY

Eleven

"Ooh, girl, school just can't let out soon enough!" Leah exclaimed as we walked down the hallway on our way to third hour.

Christmas was a few weeks away, and we would be on break soon, but that wasn't why she was excited. Today was Friday and her and Will's anniversary, so he had an entire day and night of activities he was surprising her with. He had been leaving hints in her locker all week, and now it was finally the day so she wouldn't shut up about it.

"You don't have a clue what he has planned?"

"Nope, he just told me we were staying overnight somewhere, so pack a bag."

"Do you think your momma's gonna be asking questions?"

"No. Since her and Brandon broke up, all she's been

doing is working and drinking, but if she does, I'll just say I'm with you."

"Of course, you will." I laughed as we stopped at my locker.

I put up my math book and retrieved my US History book. I already knew Will was planning to keep Leah out all day and night. Brice did too, which was the reason we'd planned to go straight to his house after school. We never got to chill there because we didn't want to risk getting caught, but since the coast would be clear today, that was precisely the plan, and we couldn't wait.

"Well, have fun! I can't wait to hear all about it."

She nodded her head as the first bell rang. Rolling her eyes, she ran off in the opposite direction toward her class. It was all the way on the other side of the school, so I doubted she would make it in time. Knowing Leah, she didn't care anyway.

* * *

School seemed to drag by, and when the bell finally rang, I bolted out of class at top speed. That was another stipulation of our sneaking around. If we wanted to meet up after school, we either had to do it down the street or rush out as soon as school was out so nobody would see us together. Usually, Brice would leave his car unlocked for me, and I would wait there until he came out of the school a few minutes later. We were typically the first ones out of the parking lot, and today was no different.

Brice made a few stops, picking up food from Chipotle,

one of my favorite restaurants, before heading back to the house. We ate and watched movies in the living room before going into the bedroom.

Hours later, we awoke to noise in the house, and I already knew it was Will and Leah.

"Shit! The fuck are they doing home?" Brice asked, jumping up and throwing on some basketball shorts. He urged me to get dressed, and when he swung open the door to get to the living room, Will was already standing there, hand up preparing to knock on the door.

"Yo," he said, the look on his face one of complete surprise seeing me half-naked in Brice's bed. The last time I was in that bed, I was being pinned down. "My bad man, didn't know you had company… or that y'all was still together."

Just when I thought it couldn't get any worse, I heard Leah from behind Will.

"What you mean 'still together'?" she quizzed loudly, pushing Will out of the way to see who was in the room. When she confirmed it was me, her whole face dropped.

"Breeon?" she boomed, shaking her head in disbelief. "Well, damn, how long has this been going on?"

I had no words to say. I was caught red-handed. You would think Leah and I were a couple, and I had cheated, but this was almost the same thing. Keeping a secret from your best friend was the ultimate betrayal, especially a best friend you had been joined at the hip with since diapers. I could see the rage on her face as she pushed Will again, but this time she was storming out of the room.

"Leah, hold on let me just talk to you!" I yelled after her, but she was hearing none of it. She went into Will's room and slammed the door so hard the house shook. I was almost scared to open it, but I did it anyway.

"Leah, I know you're mad at me—"

"Hell yeah, I'm mad at you, Breeon! Are you serious?! How long has this been going on?"

"Since a few weeks after the fight," I confessed. There was no use in lying now.

Leah rolled her eyes and shook her head so hard her hoop earrings smacked against her cheek.

"I wanted to tell you, Leah, but this is why I didn't! I knew you would be mad at me—"

"I'm not mad at you for dating Brice again. You can do what you want to do. If it's one thing I learned from my mother, it's that you can't talk a woman out of wanting to be with somebody. I'm mad because you kept it from me and didn't we just talk about keeping secrets?"

"We did—"

"And you chose to do it anyway. Because you knew I would make sure you knew that you were making a mistake."

"See what I'm talking about? This is exactly what I didn't wanna hear."

THE CENTER: BREEON'S STORY

"Nobody wants to hear that they're being stupid."

"I know you didn't just call me stupid," I expressed, completely shocked. Leah just shrugged her shoulders. "You were the one who wouldn't shut up about me giving him a chance!"

"That's how you're actin'. Wasn't Brice just cheating on you, and you took him back? I told you to give him a chance, not let him treat you like shit."

"You know what, Leah? I am so sick and tired of you acting like you are the guru on relationships! It wasn't always perfect between you and Will. He's cheated on you before too! I think you like being the one that has somebody and letting me be the third wheel."

Leah's face turned red, and I knew I had hit a nerve, but so what she had too! She had no right calling me stupid just because I was doing something she didn't agree with. What happened to no judgment?

"Damn, so you bringing that shit up, huh Breeon? I tell you something in confidence, and you just throw it in my face like that?"

"How is that any different from what you're doing? You don't mind throwing shit up in my face when it benefits your point of view, but I do it, and I'm wrong?"

"You know what, Breeon? Do what you wanna do. That's fine. Don't expect me to help you or come to your aid when he knocks your dumb ass out."

Now Leah was crossing a line, and before I knew it, I had

swung on her, nearly hitting her in the jaw.

"Bitch, I know you didn't just try to hit me!" Leah roared, getting up and pushing me with all of her strength only to fall on top of me. The boys must've heard the commotion because they ran in and separated us, Brice putting me over his shoulder.

"You are a bitch for putting your hands on me, Breeon! You better stay the fuck away from me!" Leah yelled as Brice carried me out of Will's bedroom.

"Fuck you, Leah! I don't wanna be around you anyway!" I yelled, kicking and screaming the whole way.

Brice took me home, and we sat outside in the car before I went in. Leah and I had argued before, but we'd never gotten into a physical fight. I felt terrible, but I wasn't just about to sit there and let her keep calling me dumb. I understood she was mad, but the name-calling was out of line.

"You okay?" Brice asked, rubbing the back of my neck.

"I'm still mad, but I'm just glad to be away from her."

"Yeah, Leah flew off the handle," he said, shaking his head. It was ironic that just a few months ago, I was sitting in the car with Leah having the same conversation about Brice.

"Leah has been through stuff watching her mom in her relationships, which is why she's so overprotective, but that doesn't give her the right to call me out of my name."

"Yeah, it doesn't. She was wrong for that."

THE CENTER: BREEON'S STORY

We didn't say anything for a minute. I just sat there and enjoyed the neck rub.

"Don't let this stress you out."

"Leah's my best friend, so of course, I'm gonna be stressed out."

"I'll take care of it. I'll talk to Leah and make sure she knows this was all my idea, and what happened before will never happen again. If you gave me another chance, she should be a piece of cake."

I just nodded my head because I was tired of talking about it, but I knew him making up with Leah would be easier said than done. That girl knew how to hold a grudge. I didn't know how long it was going to take for her to talk to me again.

"Go get some rest baby. I'll call you later and check on you."

Brice kissed me on the lips, and I got out of the car. Waving goodbye when I gained entry, I threw my keys on the end table and collapsed on the couch before letting the waterworks begin. I had to ask myself, was a relationship with Brice really worth the lifelong friendship I had with Leah?

Twelve

Days went by, and Leah and I didn't speak. Of course, it didn't take long for word to get back to the rest of my girls that I had gotten back with Brice, and they were equally angry. I knew I would have to face it sooner or later, and when I made it to the cafeteria the following Monday, I could already feel the tension from Kaycee and Tati.

"Hey y'all," I said, sitting in my usual chair at our table. They responded with a chorus of dry greetings.

"So, you back with Brice, huh?" Kaycee said, staring a hole through me.

"Yeah, I am. I was gonna tell y'all I swear, but I just wanted to give him a chance first to prove to me he had changed."

They were nodding their heads, but I could tell they didn't believe me. I wish they would understand that the decision I'd made was because of them and my fear of disappointing or angering them.

"And you think he has?"

"Yeah, I do. Brice has been treating me so well, and we've been getting along."

They nodded their heads, but again, they didn't believe me.

"Breeon, I know you're gonna do what you wanna do," Tati started. "But fa real, you need to be careful. We had that talk with you because we care about you. To be honest, the fact that you went behind our backs and kept dating him is like a slap in the face. You could have at least just kept it real and told us what was up."

I knew Tati was mad because as loud and boisterous as she was, she hated confrontation. Even when we'd spoken the first time about Brice, she didn't have much to say.

"Have you talked to Leah?" Kaycee asked.

I shook my head.

"Nope, and I really don't care. As far as I'm concerned, she owes me an apology for calling me out my name like she did. Until then, I have nothing to say to her."

"I mean, can't you understand where she's coming from? Even if you didn't tell us, you and Leah are like sisters."

"Because I knew nobody would understand! I mean, y'all look at Brice like he's a monster and he really ain't like that. He is sweet and treats me good most of the time—"

"That's just it, most of the time. You need to be with somebody that treats you good all the time," Kaycee stressed as if she was talking to a child. Maybe she felt like she was.

"Everything that happened in Brice's life made him like this. It's hard for him to control his anger, and sometimes he just loses control. That's not his fault, and if I love him, I can't just leave him for something that's not his fault."

"You are not his therapist, Breeon. You are not responsible for fixing him."

"I'm not trying to. I'm trying to be there for Brice because I love him."

The more I talked the more I felt like they weren't listening. It was like they weren't even trying to understand.

"I just don't wanna see you hurt, Breeon," Tati said, literally throwing her hands in the air. "I think you need to give him time to go to some anger management classes and then see if that helps."

I loved my girls, but my opinion wasn't changing. They had to understand that I needed to do some things for *myself*. They still spent the entire lunch hour giving me a mini-intervention complete with alternative options and side-eyes.

* * *

Leah and I never got into it this bad, and that was probably best because we were both stubborn, and I knew sooner or later we would be tight again, but I was banking on later unless I got my apology. I couldn't deny that I missed the hell out of her, though. We were joined at the hip, so being without her felt like I was missing my second soul.

Just when I was about to give in and go to Leah to assure her my relationship with Brice was better than ever, things took a terrifying turn. It happened late one night at the beginning of December, right before Christmas. Winter was getting off to a late start because that's how Michigan weather is, so although it was cold outside, there hadn't been any snow yet. Brice and I had been together all that day and decided to go to a late movie since I knew my dad would be working all night and wouldn't be home until early the next morning. We held hands as we exited the theater, debating whether or not the remake we'd just seen was better than the original.

"Oooh, look! Breeon's got a boyfriend. I'm telling your daddy!" I heard a voice yell out. When I looked to see who was talking about me, I spotted Man-Man's older brother Frank standing by the now vacant concession stand. I immediately went over to hug him.

"Hey, Frank! Man-Man told us you were moving home. How long you gonna be here?"

"However long it takes me to save money to get the hell outta my momma's house. Here's a word of advice. When you get the chance to move out of your daddy's house, make sure you save so you never have to come back."

"Got it," I said, laughing.

I introduced Frank to Brice, although they had seen each other before. When Brice and I proceeded to walk out, he grabbed my arm forcefully and yanked me toward the door.

"Ow, Brice, what are you doing?" I asked, trying to escape his grasp.

"Once again, you embarrassing me," he mumbled, pulling me close so only I could hear.

"What are you talking about?" I asked, genuinely confused.

"You let go of my hand to go hug on some other dude. How is that supposed to make me look?"

"It's Man-Man's brother. He's like a brother to me!"

"But he *ain't* your brother!" Brice finally yelled, his frustration taking over him and startling me all at the same time. When we made it to the car, he pushed me up against it and grabbed my neck.

"Get in this car and don't say a damn word to me. You need to learn how to act."

At this point, I was scared, but I had no other choice but to get in the car. We were on the other side of town. I didn't want to call my daddy, and Leah was the only other person with a vehicle, and of course, we weren't speaking. So I don't know if it was fear, shame, or just plain stupidity, but I got into the car and put on my seatbelt and didn't say a word just like I was told. All I needed to do was get home.

As we drove down the street, I tried my best to look at anything but Brice. We pulled up to a red light, and a car pulled beside us. The music was on full blast, and the bass was almost making Brice's car shake, so it got my attention. I glanced over, and there was a car full of boys banging their

THE CENTER: BREEON'S STORY

heads wildly. As I turned away, Brice's fist slammed against the side of my face and sent my head flying into the window. Luckily, it didn't go through.

"DON'T YOU EVER LOOK AT ANOTHER DUDE WHILE YOU WITH ME! EVER!" he yelled, spit flying out of his mouth.

As Brice's hands gripped the steering wheel and his jaw clenched, I could tell he was enraged, and I knew getting into that car had been a huge mistake. I didn't know what was about to happen before I got out of it.

I covered my face with my hands, buried my head in my lap, and cried. I couldn't believe what was happening to me. All of my friends had been right. I was getting abused, and I was ashamed that I was just now realizing it.

"I want you to shut up!" he hollered, and when I felt the car start to swing wildly, I had to peek to see what was going on. Brice had pulled the car over down a dark road, and now I really didn't know what was about to happen.

"Brice, please, take me home," I pleaded, but when I looked at him again, I didn't even recognize him. His eyes were dark, and his face was all screwed up. I slipped off my seatbelt just as he sent his hand flying across my face.

"I said shut. The. Hell. Up," he said slowly, as punches rained down on my face like a storm. Frantically, I searched for the door handle, and as soon as I opened it, I attempted to jump out, but Brice grabbed my hair.

"STOP IT BRICE!" I screamed. If nothing else, I was about to make a scene and hope a nosey neighbor looked out of their window and saw me.

    After what felt like forever, I got out of his grasp, jumped out of the car, and took off running down the street. I could hear Brice's door open, which meant he was probably chasing me, but I knew if I turned around and looked, it would slow me down. So, I cried and ran as hard and as fast as I could in search of someone that would help me.

THE CENTER: BREEON'S STORY

Thirteen

I was trying to finish telling Miss Fab the story, but I was sobbing too hard. Since the altercation had just happened, I was still shaken up. I was replaying the scene repeatedly in my head, and every time I cried. Everyone had tried to tell me, but I had gone against the people who loved me the most. Now Leah and I weren't speaking, and the rest of my girls were mad, so they had been acting shady.

Miss Gayle had arrived and was sitting next to me, rubbing my back. She was a short, brown woman with a beautiful round face and big brown eyes. Like Miss Fab, she too had dreads, and they were just touching her shoulders. She always had some dope hairpiece in her hair. This time it was a silver and blue butterfly, a gift from her son, no doubt.

Miss Fab was seated across from me, holding my hand.

"Breeon, did you tell your dad what's been going on?" she softly asked.

"No," I said, staring at the tear that had escaped my eye and landed on my hand. "I wanted to, but I knew he would be mad, and I don't want him to do anything to jeopardize his career or his freedom. He'll kill Brice."

"I understand that, Breeon," Gayle said. "But since you came here for help, and we are aware of the situation, we are required by law to inform your father."

More tears appeared. Just when I thought things couldn't get any worse. Involving my daddy meant involving the law, and that was the last thing I wanted. I wished I could just go to sleep and wake up before any of this happened. Before summer ended, before the abuse... before Brice.

"I understand," I finally said, and it was so low I didn't know if they could hear me.

"But I don't want you to be worried because I will be right there next to you every step of the way. I will be there in whatever capacity you need me to be. If you want me just to listen and let you tell him, I will. If you want me to do the talking, I'll do that too. I'm here for you."

Letting go of Miss Fab's hand, I laid on Miss Gayle's chest. At that moment, they were my angels, and I was thankful for her embrace. I imagined it was like what hugging a mother feels like. I didn't have any experience with one, but I imagined they felt like what Miss Gayle felt like. Her hugs could make everything better in your life, even on your best days. Each adult in the community center offered something, but Miss Gayle was like the heart and the glue that held it all together, just like she was doing for me at that moment.

THE CENTER: BREEON'S STORY

"Go on in my office and sit in the recliner. I'll call your father and ask him to come by."

* * *

My daddy made it to The Center in record time and had tears in his eyes as soon as he saw my face.

"What happened, baby?" he quizzed, kissing my forehead. Tears slipped down my cheeks, just seeing my father's reaction.

"Can you sit down for a minute, daddy?"

Pulling up a chair, daddy sat right next to me.

"What happened to your face, baby?" he asked again, and I could tell his reaction was changing from concern to anger.

"Mr. Bennett, Breeon was sitting on the steps this morning when I got here, and her face looked like this," Miss Fab started. "My cousin Gayle is the social worker of The Center, so I called her immediately."

Miss Gayle stood from her desk and came around it, so she was closer to us.

"Breeon confided in us and shared that she has been experiencing abuse in her relationship with Brice Foster. Last night after a date, they got into an altercation, and she was able to get away and come here."

Daddy looked at me with disbelief all over his face.

"Understand Mr. Bennett, Breeon wanted to tell you. She was afraid you would get angry and do something to jeopardize your career and your freedom. You can understand why she would be afraid to tell you."

"Yeah, I do," he said, pulling me close to him. "What happened, baby?"

I shrugged my shoulders.

"It started small. Like Brice would get mad at what I was wearing or if I talked to somebody. I thought it was because he really liked me. It was cute at first, but he started getting so mad over everything…"

I took a minute to get myself together. Now that I had started talking to him, it was all coming out so easily, and having Miss Gayle and Miss Fab there definitely helped.

"At first he pushed me, and I was like, 'no big deal, he didn't mean it' but it just got worse."

Daddy pulled me out of my seat and onto his lap. Holding me like a baby, he rocked me back and forth, wiping my tears from my eyes.

"Tell Daddy what you want done. You wanna press charges?"

I shook my head.

"I just want it to go away. I want Brice to stay away from me."

"Okay, okay, okay," he reassured. "It's gonna be okay."

Daddy talked to Miss Gayle and Miss Fab some more about steps we could take moving forward. We all agreed I

THE CENTER: BREEON'S STORY

needed to speak to a professional about what happened and take some time out of school.

Daddy and I left about an hour later, and although I was feeling sad, I was optimistic. Now that my dad knew he would surely protect me. We got into the car, and he pulled out of the parking lot. We rode in silence down the street for a while, and it took me a minute to notice we weren't going home. I didn't ask questions, though. I just sat back, closed my eyes, and let the car rock me into a light slumber.

* * *

When the car stopped, I opened my eyes and realized we were in front of a diner. Daddy got out and went in without saying a word. He emerged about fifteen minutes later with a bag of food.

"You must be hungry since you been at The Center almost all night," he said, putting the bag in my lap. It was only then that my stomach started churning. I could already smell the eggs, bacon, and sweet French toast, so I didn't waste any time opening one of the Styrofoam boxes and shoving a piece of meat into my mouth. Daddy grabbed his box , which had an all meat omelet inside. We ate for a while in silence, just watching cars go by and people in the restaurant coming and going.

"Breeon, I know we don't talk about your mother a lot," daddy said all of a sudden.

"For good reason."

"I know you hate her, but looking at you, and with everything that just happened, I think she and I both have a part in what happened with that boy."

"No, y'all don't have nothin' to do with me, daddy. I made the decisions I made. Don't blame yourself."

"I do, though," he said, shaking his head, and all of a sudden becoming enthralled by something in his box. "When I met your mother, nothing else in my life mattered. I would call in to work just to lay in bed with her all day. I knew she was married, and I knew it was wrong, but I thought I was winning her heart."

Daddy looked away and quickly wiped a tear from his eye.

"When she got pregnant with you, I was so happy. I just knew you were the answer to my prayers. You would be the reason she would leave him and finally start a life with me. However, she didn't see it that way. Once her husband found out about us, and you, she cut me off completely until she showed up at my door with you in her arms."

For a minute, he said nothing. Dad just looked out at the traffic, and then he looked at me.

"I should've been done with her then. The way she dropped you off and left...I should have moved on with my life and left her alone. I should've known then that you deserved better. But like a fool, every time she comes, I'm right there with open arms, begging and pleading for her to be a family with us. If she didn't, then why would she now?" he asked rhetorically. "No matter how long she stays away or how many times she tells me she doesn't wanna be with me, I'm still there. And maybe that's where you got it from — me allowing anything from her and not having enough backbone to stand up for myself or you. For a long time, I told myself it was all for you. I wanted you to have a mother so bad that I would do whatever it took, but it was really me and my inability to move on with my life."

I could understand the correlation my father was making. However, I still couldn't blame him, but it was like looking at myself in the mirror. Everything I said I hated about my father's attitude toward my mother was showing in how I handled my relationship with Brice. It was uncanny how we were doing the same thing, although the situation was different.

"It's hard to see the bad in someone you love, baby," he continued. "And I know you love him if you were willing to keep a secret from me, but Breeon, you have to love yourself more than you love anybody else. You gotta respect yourself enough to know when to not put up with something. I should've prepared you more for guys like Brice and how to handle them."

"Daddy, it's okay. Quit trying to make this your fault. It's on me."

"Maybe so. But maybe it also has something to do with things you've witnessed growing up. Either way, we gonna get through it. I'll let go of your mother, and you let go of Brice?"

I nodded my head, a nonverbal way of agreeing to the deal.

"And I'm proud of you for getting help."

"Thank you, daddy."

D. RENEA

He kissed me again on the forehead and looked at me. Even through all my bruises, he had the same look in his eyes he'd had that evening he was snapping all those pictures when I was on my way to homecoming. My daddy had a vision of me, and no matter what happened or what I did, nothing would ever change that.

THE CENTER: BREEON'S STORY

Fourteen

My daddy started taking me to therapy immediately. Considering I had gotten help and was distancing myself from Brice, at first, I didn't understand the need, so I didn't want to go. We got up early one morning to get to my appointment half an hour early to fill out the paperwork. When I met my therapist, I was sure there was nothing she could do for me but give me a makeup tutorial. She looked like she had just stepped off the cover of a magazine. Her makeup was flawless, and her gold and pink eyeshadow perfectly matched the pink and gold blouse she was wearing along with a black pencil skirt. She stood around 6'2, probably due to the black and pink stiletto heels she was wearing. My father was practically foaming at the mouth by the time she made it over to where we were seated.

"Mr. Bennett?" she asked, smiling and showing all of her pearly white teeth.

"Yes," he said, standing.

"My name is Lola Reed, and I'll be Breeon's therapist."

They shook hands and walked away to speak for a minute. I could tell it was about me because she kept looking over at me and smiling. When they finally came back, she stood over me, holding the clipboard to her chest.

"Hi, Breeon, my name is Lola."

"Hi," I said, forcing a smile and shaking her hand.

"We will start this session without your father, and then we'll bring him in toward the end to talk. Is that okay?"

I shrugged my shoulders, got up, and followed her to the elevator. My daddy winked at me as the doors shut and took us up to the third floor to her office. It was small, just enough space for her desk, a table and a couple of chairs. She had Marvel posters hanging around the wall, and I stared at a poster of Maya Angelou as she gathered her notebook.

Talking to Miss Reed didn't feel like an appointment. She was asking me regular questions and talking about things I enjoyed. After a while, she brought up Brice, and I started to explain the dynamics of our relationship to her. She nodded intently and took notes on her pad, and before I knew it, she was calling for them to send my father up to her office. When he arrived, he joined us at the table.

"First of all, Mr. Bennett, you have a lovely daughter. You should be very proud of her. She's smart, well-spoken, and very aware of her emotions and how to vocalize them. I'm glad that she got out of her situation before it started to affect that."

THE CENTER: BREEON'S STORY

"Thank you," my dad replied, nodding his head in agreement.

"I think keeping her out of school for a week or two is necessary. She needs to stay as far away from Brice as possible. That includes him and anybody associated with him. Sometimes when an abuser can't reach their victim, they'll use other people to get back in. Avoid that at any cost. Steer clear of his family and close friends."

This time I nodded my head.

"Now, even though she should avoid him doesn't mean she needs to isolate herself. Start being around your friends again and doing things that make you happy. It will be hard to rewire your brain to stop worrying about Brice, but this is the first step."

Miss Reed was right. Even since I'd broken up with Brice, I caught myself questioning how he would feel about what I had planned for the day or what I was wearing.

"I have no doubt that Breeon will bounce back from this with no problem. I just want to make sure she has no emotional effects in the long run. Women who have experienced abuse are more likely to suffer from disorders such as anxiety, depression, PTSD, or panic attacks, just to name a few. I also want to make sure she won't carry anything from this in her future relationships, so I would like to keep seeing her for a while."

"That won't be a problem."

I would've had to be blind not to notice how my father was hanging on to Miss Reed's every word, and it wasn't because she was the professional. He was smiling and thanking her way more than necessary and even pulled out his sexy laugh that had been reserved only for my mother. My daddy had a little crush, and I would've been lying if I said I wasn't thrilled to see it.

* * *

My phone stayed on *Do Not Disturb* my first few days at home. It was like I needed a break from everything and everyone. When I finally came back to reality, I had so many missed calls from my girls, acquaintances from school, and even Will. However, I didn't have any calls from Leah. It was going on a month now, and we still weren't speaking. At first, I was mad, but now I knew the fight had been stupid, and if it took me having to apologize for us to talk again, that is just what I would do.

I called Leah but didn't get an answer. Shrugging it off, I decided to call Raven back since she had been the one that had called the most times.

"Dang, girl! Where y'all been? Everybody just stopped coming to school and didn't tell nobody?"

"What are you talking about?" I asked, falling onto my bed and staring up at the Michael B. Jordan poster I had on my ceiling. I was gonna marry him one day.

"You and Leah ain't been at school forever. Why didn't y'all tell me y'all was playing hooky so I can join?"

"It wasn't that. I've been going through some stuff, so my daddy took me out of school. I haven't even talked to Leah."

"At all?"

THE CENTER: BREEON'S STORY

"Not since she found out I had gotten back with Brice."

"Oh... Y'all still together?"

It was crazy, but I hadn't prepared myself to answer questions about what had happened between Brice and me. I just expected people to know.

"Naw, girl, but I'll tell you about that when I see you."

I was waiting for her to object because that's how my girls were. You didn't get to decide when you would give the scoop on something, but I hoped me telling her I'd planned to tell her face-to-face would buy me some time.

"Okay, good. I tried calling Leah, but she won't pick up. Kaycee and Tati said they haven't heard from her either."

This was odd. I knew Leah was mad at me, but what was her beef with everybody else?

Raven and I chatted for a long time. Since we hadn't spoken in so long, we had a lot to catch up on. When we got off, I stared at my phone. I knew I wasn't supposed to talk to anybody close to Brice, but what if Will had called me about Leah? Or she had tried to call from his phone? Ignoring my instructions, I called him back.

"Hello?" He answered on the first ring.

"Hey Will, you call me?"

"Yeah, where you been?" he asked, making it completely obvious Brice hadn't told him about the incident. I didn't feel like talking about it.

"I just had some stuff going on, so my daddy took me out of school."

"Oh, okay. You know me and Leah broke up."

I sat up in my bed, unable to believe what I was hearing. Will and Leah were like the Jay-Z and Beyoncé of our school. Everybody knew them, were aware of their relationship, and wanted one just like it. They rarely argued and never had any scandals going on, so hearing they had broken up was a huge shock.

"Y'all didn't break up. Y'all just mad at each other, and y'all will be together again in a week."

"Not this time. I can promise you I ain't ever getting back with her ass."

"What happened?"

"I can't believe you don't know."

"Know what?" I asked, getting annoyed.

"Leah cheated on me with Brice."

Immediately I shook my head.

"No, she didn't," I said confidently. "Leah wouldn't do that to you, and she definitely wouldn't do that to me—"

"I walked in on them. I saw it. I mean, I didn't see them in the act, but she was running downstairs damn near naked, and he was right behind her. Then she gonna try to fall in my arms and apologize like I ain't know what was going on."

THE CENTER: BREEON'S STORY

Nothing about this was making sense. I know me and Leah were mad at each other, but what the hell? Was she trying to get back at me? I wanted to argue with Will some more, but how could I when I wasn't there, and he was? I was trying to picture Leah and Brice together, but it just wasn't happening for me. I couldn't believe it, and even though we weren't speaking, I had to ask her about it.

"You really ain't talked to Leah at all?" he asked.

"Nope, not since we got into it. It's weird. This is the longest we've ever gone without talking."

"Well, if I were you, I would stay away from her. She can't be trusted."

I said nothing. I just let Will's comment roll off my back. I couldn't blame him for being angry because I knew how much he loved Leah, and Brice was his best friend. However, Leah was mine, and I would never speak bad on her no matter the circumstances.

"Where has Brice been?" I asked, taking the heat off of Leah.

"Don't know, and damn sure don't care. I put him out as soon as it happened. I put his stuff on the street too, so it's a good thing he came and got it in time."

I could tell the betrayal was cutting Will deep, but I just couldn't wrap my mind around it. There had to be more to the story, and what kind of friend would I be if I didn't try to find out?

* * *

After attempting to call Leah countless times with no answer, I decided to just go to her house. She wouldn't be able to ignore me if I were right in her face. After knocking for what felt like forever, the door finally swung open, and Leah's mother Chelsea stood there wearing a pair of leopard leggings and a black tank top. Her hair was wild like she had just gotten out of bed, and it was obvious she was drunk. I could smell liquor all over her as soon as she opened her mouth.

"Hey, Bree Bree!" she greeted. She had been calling me that since I was a kid. "Where you been at, baby? I missed you! It's so good that you're here. I know Leah needs you right now."

"Just home with my daddy," I answered, ignoring the smell and hugging her.

Leah's mom had her problems, but she had always been there for me in the absence of mine. She was the one who'd taught me about what to do when I started my period and always tried to make any of my milestone events. I loved Miss Chelsea, and her addiction would not change that.

"Is Leah here?"

"She isn't. She walked to the store. You can come in and wait for her. She should be back any minute."

I came in and sat in the couch. Chelsea may have been an alcoholic, but her house stayed immaculate.

I wasn't seated long before we heard Leah come in. I went into the kitchen to meet her, and when I saw her, my mouth dropped. She was wearing sweats and had her hair pulled into a ponytail. It was weird because if there were two things that Leah hated, it was sweats and ponytails. I didn't even know she owned a pair.

"Hey, Leah," I said, breaking the month-long awkward silence between us.

"What you doin' here?" she snapped, and it caught me off guard. How could she still be mad?

"I came by to check on you."

"So you must've talked to Will," she said, putting her bag on the table and glaring at me. "That's why you here all of a sudden?"

I didn't understand why she was so standoffish. It was taking me by surprise, so I didn't know what to say. Since when did I need a reason for visiting my best friend?

"No, I just hadn't talked to you in a while... I broke up with Brice."

I actually thought that news would make her happy and kill the awkwardness, but it did just the opposite.

"So, what you want me to do? Throw you a party?"

"What is up with you, Leah?"

"*What's up with me?* I've been here for days, and you haven't had no concern, now you wanna rush over here as soon as you hear me and Will broke up?"

"I didn't—"

"You know what Bree, I'm done worrying about you and

your shit because nobody is ever there to help me deal with mine. So you, Will, and everybody else can just stay the fuck away from me and go straight to hell!"

She snatched her bag off of the counter and stormed past me so fast it made my hair blow. I just stood there, dumbfounded, unable to understand what was going on with her or what had just happened.

Fifteen

"I cannot believe y'all are still mad at me over that book!" Mrs. Hunter exclaimed with a laugh from where she was seated behind her desk. "We read that the first few weeks of school."

"Cuz that book was some BS, Mrs. Hunter," a girl named Dria said from her desk in the middle row.

"Straight BS!" Almond agreed. "You could've told us that was the way it would end. Just gonna take us by surprise like that."

Mrs. Hunter put her hand over her face and laughed. We were always giving her honest feedback on our assigned reading, but she had crossed the line with *Of Mice and Men*. Nobody expected George to kill Lennie, and that made it worse. One girl even left the class crying.

"I didn't want to spoil it for anyone. Look, that's the blessing and curse of literature…it affects everyone differently and some more than others."

We continued to go in on her until the bell rang, dismissing us from yet another day of school. I had been back for a few days, and so far, things had been going well. Of course, I saw Brice at school, but I avoided him and any eye contact anytime he was around. My father had wanted me to take out a restraining order against him, but I thought it was pointless since there was no way we could stop him from coming to school. I promised my father if he tried anything, we would do things his way.

As I exited my class, I ran into Will. His sixth hour was right across from mine. He looked sad and probably didn't even notice how low his head was hanging. He hadn't been himself, and it was showing in his demeanor and his game on the court and field.

"Hey, Will, how you doin'?" I asked, approaching him. He shrugged his shoulders.

"It is what it is. The day is over."

"Don't you got basketball practice?"

He shook his head.

"I'm not goin'."

Will never missed practice. Ever. He was taking this break up with Leah way harder than I thought, or he had other stuff going on.

"Wanna hang?" he asked as we approached his car.

"I don't know—"

THE CENTER: BREEON'S STORY

"Come on, Bree, you ain't got nothing else to do, and I need somebody to cheer me up."

Will was wrong. I did have stuff to do...like a six-page English paper that was due next week. He was right about needing someone to cheer him up. It was all over his face and had been all day.

"Okay, I'll hang today and work on my paper tomorrow," I said as I got in the passenger side of the car. "And you coming to the library with me while I get it done too."

When we walked in Will's house, it was obvious something had happened because it was stuff everywhere, even more than usual. It was obvious someone had moved out because there were empty spots where all of Brice's belongings used to be. Aside from that, beer and liquor bottles were everywhere. Tiptoeing through the trash on the floor, I made my way to the couch while Will disappeared into the kitchen. He emerged just seconds later, carrying two unopened bottles of liquor.

"Let's play a game," he said with the first smile on his face I had seen all day.

"What game? What are you doing? Where did you get that liquor? You not even old enough to buy alcohol."

"Daaamn, you sound like my momma, Bree. Relax a little. It's Friday, we ain't got school tomorrow, and my life sucks. All good reasons to drink."

"I ain't ever really drank liquor," I admitted to him, ignoring his comment about his life.

After seeing what liquor had done to Leah's mother, it kind of scared me. Other than a sip of my Daddy's beer or wine every now and then, I never drank.

"I thought you didn't either."

"I didn't. Not until your best friend tore my heart out my chest, and my *ex*-best friend stomped all over it. Now, it's all I wanna do."

He tipped the bottle up to his lips and took a long drink of the clear liquid.

"Anyway, fuck all that... We about to have fun."

He ran back into the kitchen and got two plastic shot glasses that looked like little red plastic cups. Sitting back on the couch, he filled each one until they were almost overflowing.

"Okay, let's play Two Truths and a Lie. Pretty self-explanatory. I say three things, and you guess which one is the lie. If you wrong, you drink."

"Okay, that sounds easy," I said, putting my feet on the couch and getting comfortable. Will and I had known each other since elementary, so I figured there weren't much about him I didn't know. "You go first."

"Okay," he said and paused as he thought for a minute. "I dribbled my first basketball when I was two... my family was poor when I was born and... my great uncle once caught a 50-pound fish."

THE CENTER: BREEON'S STORY

"Man, that's not fair! All of those could be true."

"Yeah, that's the point, Breeon. You thought I was gonna make it easy for you?"

I rolled my eyes as I thought for a minute. Two seemed a little young to be dribbling a basketball, but then as far as I knew, Will's family had never been poor. I just couldn't decide if a fish could really be 50 pounds.

"I think the fish one is the lie. Can a fish really weigh 50 pounds?"

"Actually, it was 53 pounds," he said grinning. "Bottoms up."

I sighed as I picked up the cup, the liquid spilling down my fingers. I took a deep breath before drinking the liquid and groaned at the taste as I swallowed it. The face I was making must have been ugly because Will was laughing so hard that he had tears in his eyes.

"I witnessed Breeon Bennett take her first shot of liquor. I'm honored."

I laughed and stuck up my middle finger at him. It wasn't amusing.

"Anyway, it's my turn."

I paused for a minute to think. This would be hard, considering Will's ex was my best friend and probably told him more than she should.

"Okay. I had my first kiss when I was five... I have a birthmark underneath my right breast... and my little cousin threw me in the pool when I was two."

Will looked at me with a blank face.

"I don't know why I thought this would be easier. I would say the pool one is the lie."

"Nope, the birthmark one. Drink up, buddy."

Will shook his head and shrugged his shoulders. But instead of grabbing a shot glass, he grabbed the entire bottle, turned it up, and took a few big gulps like it was nothing. I just shook my head with my mouth wide open.

We played about seven rounds of 2 Truths and a Lie, and I lost every one of them. By the time we were done, my body felt so light, and I was so carefree. Since we were both tipsy, we acted like kids trying to find any and everything to get into. After having an impromptu dance battle, we both collapsed on the couch, out of breath.

"Damn, I'm tired as hell," I complained. I could barely see because my eyes were so low, and I had a feeling that I wouldn't be moving again anytime soon.

"That's because you were dancin' your ass off."

"You already know I love me some Cardi B! I can't help but shake my ass when she comes on."

I bust out rapping the lyrics to Cardi B's "Money" like I was in the recording booth. I knew every single word. Will was just watching me and shaking his head, and then I felt him moving closer. When he wrapped his arm around me, I didn't even pay it any attention. We were friends, and it wasn't the first time he had his arm around me.

THE CENTER: BREEON'S STORY

"Breeon," he said in a low whisper.

I didn't answer. The liquor had me feeling dizzy, and therefore I didn't open my eyes. Maybe if I did, I would've seen Will lean in and kiss me on the lips, and perhaps it wouldn't have felt so good. Maybe I would've remembered that he was my best friend's man and we were crossing a line. At that moment, though, I wasn't thinking about any of that. It had been so long since I had been kissed and touched like this, which probably was why I kissed him back and pulled him in closer. He was hurting, and I was hurting too, but this was still very wrong.

He stopped kissing me, and I opened my mouth to tell him to stop.

"Will, this isn't right," I slurred, but made no attempt to stop him as he lifted my shirt over my head.

"I know," he replied without taking his eyes off of me. "We shouldn't do this."

His words didn't match his actions either, because he covered his lips with mine again, sliding his tongue in my mouth. The room started spinning. I opened my mouth again, but the only thing that came out was a moan as Will fingered me through my panties and kissed me.

No way could this go any further. We had to stop...

* * *

The bells rang over and over in my head, and I was so confused.

What the fuck is that noise, and why isn't anybody turning it off? I asked in my head.

"Daddy?" I called out, half asleep, my eyes still closed. Whatever it was he was doing, he needed to stop. My head was killing me.

There was silence for a minute, and then those damn bells again! Slowly my brain began to wake, and I remembered what those bells were.

My phone!

I sprang up and immediately grabbed my head to stop the room from spinning.

Where the hell am I? I thought as I closed my eyes again to stop the pounding in my head. When I opened them, I gasped as my eyes scanned the room swiftly.

"Oh my gosh!" I exclaimed, grabbing Will's shirt and doing my best to cover myself. "Oh my gosh, what the hell did I do?"

Tears slid down my face as I tried to rethink what had happened the night before that led up to Will and me ending up naked together on the couch.

Again, my phone rang loudly, and I looked down and saw my dad's face on the screen. It was almost two in the morning, and I wasn't home. I knew he was about to trip, but I had no choice but to answer the phone.

"Breeon Angelica Bennet! Where the hell are you?" he screamed in my ear.

"Daddy, I am so sorry. I fell asleep."

THE CENTER: BREEON'S STORY

"Where the hell are you, Breeon?"

I didn't know what to say. He would trip if I told him I was at Brice's, I couldn't expect Leah to lie for me with the way our relationship had been. And what would I do if she asked me where I was?

"Daddy, I'm at Raven's, and I fell asleep," I lied. Raven lived the furthest away, so he couldn't just come and pick me up. "I'm so sorry, daddy. It was a mistake."

"Get your ass home right now!"

He hung up, and I immediately started shaking Will out of his drunken slumber.

"Will, wake up!" I yelled.

"Yo, what the hell?" He asked blinking.

It took him a minute, but finally, he sat up on the couch in his boxers, looking as lost as I felt. Crossing my arms and glaring at him, I asked him two questions:

"What did we do, and how the hell are we gonna tell Leah?"

Discussion Questions

1. What is the problem faced by the main character of this story?

2. What warning signs did Brice display when he started dating Breeon?

3. What steps should Breeon have taken to avoid/end the relationship with Brice?

4. In the book Leah told Breeon "as long as he doesn't hit you don't worry about it." Is this true? Would you give this advice to your friend?

5. Do you think Breeon's father's relationship with her mother played a part in her decisions when dating Brice?

6. In what ways did the community center help the youth in the community?

7. What would you do if you had a friend who was abusing someone?

8. What should you do if you experience abusive behavior from your boyfriend/girlfriend, or know someone else who is?